# THE RUNNING OF WOLVES

## NATHAN M. BOWIE

*To my parents, for always loving me, supporting me and believing in me. To describe you as amazing will always be an understatement and I owe you much more than a dedication for all the sacrifices you both have made for me.*

# CHAPTER 1

## THE RUNNING OF WOLVES

The wolves were running again in the dark and shrouded forest of Malcoren. This forest stood not ten miles from the town stead of Little Carr, yet it was still mostly unexplored and uninhabited by men. This was mainly due to the many stories that had built up around the forest. Every child knew them by heart; they were never nice stories with princesses and knights, but always about evil creatures who would eat little children who didn't obey their parents. The adults would always laugh at the stories which, they too, were told in their childhood, but they'd avoid the wood all the same, even walking many extra miles to avoid it. This night, as a full moon shone down upon it, the forest looked particularly sinister.

Yet for a desperate father and his daughter who clung to him these stories weren't enough to deter them. As their grey horse raced through the close trees, these old legends danced in their heads, but they were far past fear of stories. The stories had already come to life.

Their horse broke through the foliage at breakneck speed, as if the poor beast knew that something was following them. The entire journey to the woods, the Father had been comforting his daughter with kind words and smiles, but now he wore a grim look and no sound slipped through his mouth. He knew that Daisy wasn't an easily spooked horse, so he held fast to his beloved child and the reins and kept his eyes forward not daring to see what was behind him.

It wasn't long before the howls started.

It was a call to the hunt that any wolf would know and come running to meet. It echoed throughout the entire accursed forest, spreading throughout every tree, every hollow. The wolves were running, and they wouldn't stop until their prey was in between their teeth. Every living thing within the forest knew not to get in the way of the bloodshot eyes of the pack, every creature knew to stay silent and hush their small ones. For blood would be spilt that night.

There was a silence that the father knew not to trust, but all he could do was wordlessly urge his horse onward, clinging to a fool's hope and a small axe, meant for wood cutting. But it was sharp and with enough force could do enough damage. He hoped.

Then a beating started, just a faint one, just like the small beat of the man's young daughter's heart. But it became louder and louder, until it seemed as if the shadows created by the trees were the ones producing it. It was the beating pulse of many paws on the forest floor. Coming ever closer, their blood thirsty eyes stared through the dark at their prey. To the wolves, there was nothing else in the world but the horse, the father and his daughter.

The first of the wolves came into the father's vision. It ran with a ferocity and speed that caught him off guard, but he soon righted himself. He needed to survive. He needed to get to *him*. The white coated wolf, its fangs sharp and gleaming in the moonlight made one last push of speed and leapt forward, its mouth wide with intent.

Its mouth was not met with the warm flesh of the horse, but with the slashing of the cold steel from the father's axe. The wolf fell back with a whimper, but it was soon replaced by two more wolves, snarling their even larger fangs at him. He now looked around, noticing that the horse was flanked on both sides by large white wolves, their eyes full of hunger and the impulse of the hunt.

The father felt the panic rush up his back, knowing that if he didn't do anything these wolves would surely make short work of him, but worse, his daughter. He pulled the reins to the side in a sharp motion, pushing Daisy to her right. As she swayed to the right, his axe swiped at the wolves which came into reach, being met with snarls, but also more crimson on the already blood-stained axe.

The horse kept her pace, even galloping faster than her already pushed pace, as the fangs of the wolves snapped at her legs. They sped forward, weaving in and out of the dark trees which sprang up from the ground seemingly out of nowhere. The terrain was traversed half by the adrenaline-filled man at the reins, and half by the natural instinct of the horse. Both horse and rider were desperate, the need to survive filled their blood stream.

The wolves leapt and snapped and were met with the unskilled swings of an axe. Sometimes these wild swings met the wolves as they jumped up, other times it simply cut the air. The hunt was still very much on for the wolves, and they weren't about to be discouraged by a few cuts. Their hunger was more to them that.

The father felt fear rush throughout him and clutched his crying daughter to his chest with one hand but used the other to keep on swinging for his life. A flash of white came to his left-hand side, and he quickly swapped the hand his axe was in, while only letting go of his daughter for a moment. Without hesitation, he swung out with his axe again where he'd seen the flash of white. It met the wolf's open mouth, but instead of being easily pulled away, it gripped onto it, with a might that almost pulled the man's arm off. He made a split-second decision - let go or be pulled off - and so he let go of his lifeline.

"Father?" asked the man's daughter looking up at him with eyes full of tears, and it broke his heart to see her eyes look up at him.

He forced himself to keep his head upright and take the reins by both hands, kicking the horse in the belly to push her forward. He let a single tear fall down his cheek, and he knew that it may be the last one he ever shed.

He was aware of the wolves at his feet, and deep down knew that no matter how much he pushed the horse, the wolves would always be faster, and the hunt would only end one way: the prey being devoured by the pack. Yet he still urged the horse forward, hoping beyond hope that something or someone would save them, that his daughter would have a full life before her, rather than a one that ended at the teeth of the savage creatures that were chasing them.

They kept on running and the wolves chased with a new drive of hunger in their snarls. One large wolf, as white as a new fall of snow and an ugly scar down one eye, made a dive at the horse's leg and its mouth closed around the grey flesh. The horse gave a yelp and fell to its side, throwing the man and his daughter to hard forest floor.

As soon as he was able, the man crawled to his daughter, who lay on the forest floor now crying silently. He could tell that she was too scared to make a sound, and he could not blame her. He held her in his arms and put her face to his chest, allowing her tears to be soaked up by his wool coat. He could hear the sounds of the horse being finished off by the wolves, he didn't hear how many, but the horse's pained whinnies didn't last long, but they were haunting enough, especially when he knew that it would be his screams to fill the air next.

"F…F…Father," he heard his daughter say through fearful tears.

"Amys…Amys. I'm here. Your father isn't going to let anything bad happen to you," he said.

But everything in him told him what a terrible father he was. He should've never been persuaded to take her with him, and now he'd lead her to their deaths. He held her close to him, and he looked around him and only saw red eyes in the darkness surrounding them. They were surrounded, but the wolves seemed to be waiting for something.

"Are we going to see Mummy soon?" asked Amys.

She held onto him with the most heart-breaking grip a young girl could give, her head still nuzzled into his chest.

"Very soon, my love. Very soon…" he replied letting his words trail off.

If there was an afterlife like the priest said, there was no way he would be able to look his wife in the eye, never mind whatever else there was up there.

The red eyes of the wolves surrounded both figures, waiting for something. Then one of the larger wolves stepped forward, so that the man could see the outline of its white coat and muscular physique. It started walking and then bounded, leaping toward him. The man braced for the pain which was to come, holding to his daughter for what he thought would be the last time.

But the pain never came, and the man opened his eyes to see the wolf that he'd last seen diving toward him mouth wide open, now lying on its side, a bolt deep in its eye, and its white fur twitching, the life quickly leaving its large body. All around him there were howls of anger from the wolves, but the father's eyes were fixed on the bolt which seemingly had come out of nowhere.

"What's happening?" asked Amys' small voice.

"I... I... I don't know," he replied with absolute honesty.

Just then a lot of things happened, all at the same time. Three pinecones burning with fire flew out of the darkness, each one lighting up the directions they flew in, revealing the many wolves around them. When they landed, they caught on the dry ground instantly, and spread just as quickly. A panic set in amongst the wolves, as they all began howling and running in different directions, as the fire blazed around them, spilling onto their fur coats and setting them alight. Two wolves jumped through the now spreading flames and bared their teeth at the man and his daughter, and he attempted to stand to his feet, but he couldn't in time and the wolves were already coming closer.

Out of the darkness leapt a cloaked figure, landing between the hunters and their prey. His cloak was dark like the rest of his clothing and leathers. The father didn't get a proper look at his face when he leapt out of the darkness, but he could see a greying stubbly beard poking out from under the hood. In one hand, he held a sword, a thin blade with a complex guard, interwoven metal to create a safety from other weapons. In the other, the man held a dark metal buckler, well-kept, but old with use. This was a man who had seen battle before and knew the tools of war. This was exactly whom the man who held onto his daughter was looking for.

The hooded figure wasted no time. He thrust his sword into the left side of the wolf's head, spilling blood and resulting in a yelp of pain. The other wolf leapt forward, but the metal buckler stopped any damage that the teeth of the wolves might have inflicted. The figure kicked the wolf off his sword, and quickly pushed the tip of the steel into the other wolf, who went down howling. He gave one last blow to the other, and then turned to face the man and his daughter.

He looked quite the figure, with fire all around him, blood dripping from his blade and the howls of wolves echoing all around them. This was not a man that even an accursed forest would want to have as an enemy.

"If you want to live, come with me," said a gruff voice from inside the hood.

The cloaked figure then grabbed the man by the arm and pulled him up, with a surprising strength. Amys began crying again, her tears reflected the fire burning all around them.

"Can you run with her in your arms?"

"Y-y-yes"

"Then do it," the cloaked figure said and then began to run into the woods.

Before the man knew what he was doing, he was following, his daughter in his arms, running away from the fire and the deathly howls of the wolves. He kept the figure always in his sight, holding onto his daughter throughout.

They ran in and out of the now darker and darker trees, leaping over dead foliage and small streams. The forest was dark and sinister, reflecting the way it was described in the stories with the tall fir trees staring down at them with nightmarish intent. The man felt his lungs burning, but he did not stop running; he knew he could not. Not for his sake, but for his daughter's. If this got them away from the danger he had got them into on a fool's errand, running was the least he could do.

After what seemed like hours but might have just been minutes, they came upon the outline of a horse. It was black, blacker than the night surrounding them, action-worn like her master, bearing worn hooves and strong legs made for running. The father took a moment to breathe and fill his lungs with the stuffy air of the woods.

"Put the girl on the horse and get on yourself," ordered the figure in a voice that demanded obedience.

Breathlessly, the father placed his daughter onto the horse, then got on himself, taking extra care to make sure that the child was safely between his arms. They may have escaped from the wolves, but they weren't safe yet. The hooded figure whispered something into the horse's ear and then walked around to the father.

"Ride. She knows where she's going," said the gruff voice.

Before the father could interject, the man hit the horse on its rear end and set them off riding. The last the father saw of the cloaked figure that evening was him standing in the moonlight watching them ride away.

That final leg of the journey was a blur for the father who held onto his daughter for dear life. He noticed nothing apart from the constant up and down motions of the horse racing forward through the forest. He did remember the trees slowly opening up into a clearing where there was a small grassy hill, which led up to a stone cottage at the base of a mountain. Relief and exhaustion flooded into him as the horse slowed down and plodded slowly up the hill.

He didn't remember falling off the horse onto the soft grass, his daughter landing softly onto him. He never could recall the hooded figure returning many hours later and carrying them both into the firelit cottage. But he always remembered the sounds of the white wolves' howls from the fire.

## CHAPTER 2

## THE MEN ON HORSEBACK

*A* full sun shone down on the sleepy village of Tindale, a blue and clear sky indicating the heat of the summer months. On a hot day like this, villagers would normally be outside selling their various wares. The farmers from the surrounding farmhouses would be stripped to their waist, completing tasks that they could only carry out in weather like this, like fixing roofs or doing that one thing their wives had been asking them to do all year long. However, today the village folk and the people from the surrounding farms were all stuffed into the small church building. They were waiting curiously, uneasily to hear whatever the men in armour who rode into the village had to say.

It wasn't often that Tindale had visitors apart from small time merchants or travellers passing through. Any strangers on horseback coming in the King's name was a surprise and a shock, and nobody in their right mind would miss hearing what they had to say. They had come in the morning, a group of five men wearing armour, riding on large horses. These types hadn't been seen in that area for many years. The leader, a tall thin man with a long nose had enquired of the mayor. After only a few minutes of talking, the mayor called a town meeting, and so within hours, the entire village and nearby countryside knew of the meeting and were now in attendance.

The tall, skinny man, who went by the name of Sergeant Cleaver, stood at the front of the church looking down at the gathered crowd, sweating profusely through his mail. There was a lulled silence, as every man, woman and child were eager not to miss a single word. Farmers stood to the sides of the pews, wiping sweat from their foreheads with clothes, their wives and children sitting in the pews nervously, the summer heat becoming oppressive.

"Ahem…" Sergeant Cleaver cleared his throat, preparing to speak in his refined city voice.

"A message from the High King Al-cander, first of his name, son of King Alexander II the Conqueror, son of Meli-cander, the daughter, the Queen of Fire, and your King," began the Sergeant, his voice high-pitched, painful to the hearers' ears, like a squeaky door hinge.

There were murmurs when the name Melicander was mentioned. The word "witch" was thrown around in whispers when the queen mother was mentioned, but overall, it wasn't a such a bad way to start the notice.

"The bastard and usurper Alexander has attempted to take the kingdom that is rightfully mine by the blood right of my father. He has used the army of heathens from the land of Tagon and taken land that is rightfully mine," spoke out the Sergeant.

Much of this news was new to the villagers. They had heard bits and pieces from the few people that passed through the village. There were gasps from the villagers as the words were spoken, looking at each other with pale worried faces. But they hadn't the worst of it yet.

"My advisers and her Highness, the Queen Mother, have recommended that I make a push against the traitor and take back the land that belongs to me. This requires manpower. I gave an order to the lord responsible for the villages and towns that this letter is addressed to, Lord Bradley, who has thus far left this order dormant."

The mention of Lord Bradley also stirred murmurs from the villagers. Lord Bradley was the portly lord of the manor. The village of Tindale lay on the edge of his land. For a long time, the village had not seen patrols of his constables or judges, and sometimes even the taxmen had missed their deadlines. The villagers always assumed that this was because they were on the very edge of the land, but this was merely a guess. It wasn't the first time the village was neglected by a lord, and that's the way they preferred it.

"That is why I, your High King, now call on all men who can carry a sword to come to the capital and join the grand army of the High King to push back the traitors. Any man who does not accompany the heralds sent to escort to the men to the capital, will be hung on grounds of cowardice. Signed by High King Al-cander," finished the Sergeant.

There was silence for a moment. But not for long. There followed an uproar from the villagers.

Wives held onto their husbands and sons, weeping loudly. Men stood tall holding their wives to their chests, scared and grim. Many of these men had not left the village in their entire lives, and now they had to go to war. The children screamed, not quite knowing what was going on, only aware of the tension of the crowd. The only one who seemed not panic was Tristan, who wore an excited smile.

Tristan was an older youth with shaggy light brown hair, and keen brown eyes. He was tall for his age, and he was also well-built from work on his grandparent's farm. He had never left that farm, apart from visiting Tindale for supplies, celebrations and to see Isabella. This was his opportunity to make a life for himself, and what's more a war could make him a hero. And the chance to make a name for himself, something that came only once in a lifetime. This is what he needed, and he could feel himself walking forward through the panicking crowds. Although his heart ached at the thought of leaving his grandparents, he knew he had to grasp it.

"Enough of this. Men - take the women and children outside, then we can see what kind of men this backward dump creates," shrieked the Sergeant, pointing toward the crowds.

Tristan could see the mayor try to say something to the sergeant. But his words were ineffective, falling on deaf ears. The four other soldiers, tall men with dour faces, moved through the building, systematically pulling the women away from their husbands, and carrying children to the church doors. Tristan was thankful that he was sorted with the men who were ordered to stay behind. This would be his opportunity. He felt a sting though when he saw his grandparents being asked to leave. The last thing he saw of them were the big oaken doors shutting on their worried and pale faces.

What remained was around thirty men of a range of ages - certainly not a grand army. Many of them had seen too many winters, their beards grey and their heads balding. There were two or three men in their late twenties and early thirties who looked like they might be fit enough to hold a weapon and use it with the strength necessary to do any kind of damage. But they weren't warriors, they were farmers. Most of the young men left the village before their twenty first birthday anyway, and those who remained were home loving, not exactly soldier material.

Tristan, of course, didn't think for a second that he might one of those unprepared for battle.

The only person in that group of men whom Tristan had ever seen carrying a sword was a man in his early twenties from Pickland who had moved to a vacant farm not two summers ago with his wife, who strangely was from Malancore. He had never interacted with either of them. But it did occur to him in that moment that both nations seemed to be very far away from each other, but this thought was pushed from his mind as more ideas of future glory flooded in. These thoughts kept his mind occupied as he looked ahead at the long-nosed sergeant, who was gathering himself, facing the new recruits with a look of unsurprised disappointment.

"You who are gathered here today are now all in the compulsory employment of the Crown. You have this evening to gather anything you need for the road to the capital. Bring any weapons that you may have in your possession and say goodbye to your families. We meet at sunrise in the town square. Any absences will be noted, and they will be punished as the King ordered," announced Sergeant Cleaver.

Without further ceremony, he stepped down and marched out, the mayor rushing after him. The large oak doors were opened by soldiers, and they were met by the anxious faces of the crowd.

Tristan walked out in a daze, surrounded by other men who ran to their families weeping. His grandparents rushed to him as fast as their old bones would allow, questioning him about what had occurred inside the building. All he could do was mumble something about joining the army and needing to be in the town square by sunrise. Their reaction was the same as all the others, weeping and holding onto him tightly. He didn't really notice the tears, as his head was filled with thoughts being a hero and a warrior.

As the crowds dispersed back to their homes, more sober than when they had arrived, Tristan could not help thinking about all that he was going to do and achieve. He supposed that he would likely be picked out as a special talent from the other young men, perhaps even be given his own command. Suitably boyish thoughts. It was all going be like the stories he'd grown up on.

As he imagined the King awarding him riches beyond his imagination and placing a golden circlet on his head, his grandparents held him close, one to each side of him. Their tears wetted his shoulders as they leaned on him, walking all the way to the farmhouse they called home.

# CHAPTER 3

## THE HOUSE IN THE GLADE

*A*mys' eyes snapped open as soon as the light touched them. She had always been an early riser, especially on days when her father wasn't working. She strongly believed in making the most of each day, something she vaguely remembered her mother telling her. But she couldn't say for certain if it really had happened. Memories of her mother were sketchy.

She immediately noticed that she was in an unfamiliar bed, lying next to her father whose gentle snores told her that he was still sleeping. Although Amys would normally wake her father up with great exuberance, she thought better than that this morning, deciding that exploring was her top priority. Looking about her, the bed seemed to be in a hollow of sorts in the side of a house, with a blanket separating the sleeping quarters from the rest of the room. The blanket itself was coarse and grey, but a chink of light still penetrated it so that Amys could make out the outlines of things on the other side.

She slipped under the covering and out of the bed, sliding the short way down on her front, being very careful indeed not to wake up her father. As soon as her feet touched the wooden floor, she spun around to take in her new environment. It was a single room, round, with a table in the middle. What was immediately apparent to her was how messy the room was, and she knew if her Auntie Jackie was there, she would have described it as a 'right royal mess'. The table itself was a confusion of used cutlery and plates, half cut vegetables and crumbs of bread. The floor was mud strewn. There was a wooden chest of sorts that seemed to have also been used as a way of scraping mud off boots evidenced by a dry brown line covering the underside of the lid.

It was a mess and Amys decided that she would take it upon herself to fix it.

She decided the first thing to do was clear the table and wash the dishes. She looked around the room for a sink of sorts and ended up finding a water bucket near the fireplace. The fire was still going and since she wanted to avoid any accidents with flames, she dragged the bucket a few steps away, only spilling some of it on the way. She, however, figured this would aid in the eventual washing of the floor.

She was not tall enough to reach all the table properly to be able to do any effective clearing. So, she pulled one of the three chairs from around the table, and scrambled up it to reach as many of the dishes and cutlery as she felt she needed to take care of. She had to take multiple journeys up and down the chair. This was due to a combination of her lack of strength to carry many things at a time and her awareness that her journey up and down the chair could be full of perils to crockery. By the time she was finished, she had managed to get as many dirty dishes as she could see into the water bucket.

The next thing to find was something she could use to wash the dishes with. She guessed there would be no soap, but at the very least she figured there may be a cloth of some kind she could use to wipe off the mess of dried food and crumbs. She looked all over the room her eyes peering around for a cloth or even a rag. The house was definitely well lived in and for some time and yet it was sparsely furnished. The table and chairs were the only furniture; there didn't seem to be much in the way of clothes and there was certainly nowhere to wash. After some time, she managed to find a rag underneath the bed that was covering a small chest, likely to avoid it getting dusty. But Amys wasn't concerned with the chest itself, she was just thankful she could get started on the task set before her.

Amys became very engrossed in her task. She carefully dunked each dull coloured plate or food covered cutlery into the bucket of water, using the rag to wipe away any sign of use, and then carefully she placed it to her side. She started humming a song to herself and slowly a respectable number of dishes built up beside her. She was so engrossed that she didn't hear the sound of a horse trotting up to the house. She wasn't aware of the sound of someone jumping off their steed and walking up to the house. However, she became very quickly aware of the presence of someone else when the door to the house opened letting in the fresh air.

She quickly dropped the dish that she was painstakingly washing and instinctively backed away from the bucket to see the new arrival. He was grizzled looking man, with a wide chest and an unshaven grey beard. His hair was dark but greying, cut short on the sides, but growing freely on the top of his head. His eyes were dark, made darker from the light streaming in behind him creating a shadow around his form. He wore a cloak that ended around his knees and a scowl on his face.

"What are you doing?" demanded a gruff voice.

Amys feared the voice; it sounded accusing and angry.

However, she did also note it was surprisingly level for an adult who seemed on verge of giving her a rebuke.

"Washing the dishes," she squeaked, holding her dress up to her face so that it was covered, so that she didn't have to look at the man's face while she was being told off.

But the anticipated telling off never came; all the man did was take off his cloak and trail some more mud as he went towards the bucket. He knelt down at the already washed dishes. Sighing, he picked them up and placed them back onto the table.

"I suppose they needed washing anyway," he said making a return journey for the cutlery and also putting it onto the wooden table.

"You're not angry?" blurted out Amys.

She slowly released her dress from her face, tilting it to one side wondering what the strange man would do next. He grunted a negative response to her inquiry and walked towards the bed, the water bucket in his hand. She gazed on, a little mesmerised as he pulled back the curtain and sat next to the sleeping body of her father. That was when the last night's events came back to her and she felt overwhelmed with the deep fear that had shot through her the night before. She was, however, used to not crying, because crying made her father remember her mother, and that always made him sad, so she bit her lip while the man put a cloth that she had somehow missed in her search onto her father's head.

"Will Father be all right?" she asked.

Amys was so concerned that she didn't even think about the recipient of the question.

"He will be fine; he just needs to rest," reassured the gruff man as he stood up from the bed and walked back to the door, bucket in hand.

This action reminded Amys that the man was strange and

she unthinkingly backed away two steps. But, very soon after, she found the courage to shuffle forward the equivalent of four steps.

"Are you going out?" inquired Amys looking past the man's body and spotting a beautiful black horse standing outside.

She inadvertently let out a gasp when she saw the beautiful creature, its black coat reflecting the sunlight as it shook its mane. The gruff man followed her eyeline to the beautiful beast, and let himself smile, his eyes looking to the ground as if there was something that brought back a fond memory there.

"Well - it appears I need to get more water," he remarked.

He pulled up the bucket into Amys eyeline, but she forgot to be embarrassed; she only had eyes for the horse. He started to step out of the house and Amys couldn't help but let out a little sound of disappointment.

"You could come with me if you'd like..." he invited with much hesitation.

Amys didn't give him the chance to take the statement back. She felt her heart beating inside of her chest as she threw her shoes on and rushed past him. Many horses came through Little Carr, but she had never seen one as elegant as this one.

As she rushed out, Amys felt a stab in her heart and turned back to look at the bed that she knew her father was lying on. She wanted to go riding on the horse, but if something bad happened to him it really wasn't worth thinking about.

"Are you absolutely sure he will be all right?" she asked looking up at the man, who was now outside and in the sunlight he didn't look half as bad as she thought he was at first.

However, his face was set in a stern expression, as if he wasn't used to having anyone around to smile at.

"Like I said, he'll be fine, he just needs rest. Now would you like a ride on Izzy or not?" asked the man gruffly but not rudely, Amys was sure of that - it just came out a bit roughly, a little like the way his greying stubble poked out of his cheeks and chin.

This was all Amys needed to run up to the horse, stroking and doting on the beast. She made many sounds of excitement and little giggles that only little girls are capable of making. The horse didn't seem impressed by what she was doing, but Amys didn't notice because she was already in love with her. All the horse seemed to do was give a death stare to the man, and in reply to this, shrugged and lifted Amys, still in a state of absolute bliss, onto the horse's back. He soon joined her. With one swift action, he was behind her, but she only half noticed as she now had a new access to the neck of the horse and took full advantage.

"Are you ready?" asked the man and she nodded with enthusiasm.

With that, they were off at a gallop.

To Amys, it seemed like they were flying, gliding through the very air around them as it brushed past her face. She marvelled at the elegance of the movement of Izzy's legs, seeming hardly to touch the ground. The grass that Izzy was running through didn't seem to notice her either as if blew back and forward in the soft breeze, as each individual blade basked in a sun beam of its very own. The little breeze seemed more akin to a wind storm to Amys from her position on Izzy's back, but she didn't mind one bit and she couldn't help but smile broadly.

As soon as the wonderful gallop had started, it finished, as Izzy slowed down from her gallop into a more restrained canter and then stood perfectly still by a well. The well was made of simple cut rock built three high and in a circle. Above the circle, there were two wooden beams supporting the rope used to lower the bucket and a small roof to cover the water beneath from the full force of the elements.

The man jumped off the horse and began getting the bucket ready to lower the bucket down the well. Amys stayed on the horse and continued her rubbing of Izzy, but as she did, she took in her surroundings.

"So, if your horse's name is Izzy, what is your name?" probed Amys.

She peered into forest line that was just beyond the well. The forest itself didn't seem so bad in the light of day, but she remembered some of the stories that Henry and Stephan told her and held onto Izzy's coat a little tighter.

"I've had many names in my life," replied the man.

He focused on attaching the bucket to a hook at the end of the rope and began the process of gently lowering it down. Amys also thought he muttered something else about not all of the names being nice, but she wasn't sure if she'd just made that up.

"What's your real name though? The one your mother gave you?" persisted Amys sitting upright on the horse looking directly at the man.

He stopped lowering the rope for a moment and looked up at the very steep incline that was on the other side of the glade. He was silent for a moment, and Amys hoped she hadn't said anything wrong, but all she'd asked was his name.

"What do you think my name should be?" he grunted, finally breaking the silence and his eye contact with the trees.

Amys thought about this for a moment, and then giggled to herself when she had thought of the perfect name.

"I think your name should be Pip."

"Pip? It sounds like the name of a cat," he replied glancing at her for a moment, with the hint of a smile on his face, as he turned back to his task.

"That's because it is the name of a cat," said Amys her arms folded and nodding with all the seriousness she could muster with a smile beginning to dance around her lips. From this reply she thought perhaps she heard something like a laugh, but it may have just been the wind.

"Why do I remind you of a cat?" the man asked his back still turned to her, his voice disinterested.

"Well - one of my neighbours has a ginger tom cat called Pip. He is old and can be very grumpy, but when you get to know him, he's very soft on the inside."

She smiled at him disarmingly, and he looked over his shoulder with even larger hint of a smile on his face.

"So, I remind you of an old and grumpy ginger cat."

He fully smiled, and now Amys realised why he didn't smile often - he wasn't very good at it. But she decided it was better to not tell him that at this moment in time.

"But, soft on the inside."

"Well, then Pip it is. Grumpy old man Pip."

He chuckled to himself as the bucket reached the water at the bottom of the well.

Amys looked at Pip for a bit longer, and more she looked the more he really did remind her of the neighbour's cat. When they had first got that cat, she knew that she was going to be friends with it, whether he liked it or not. After a little time, and some treats, and more than few scratches, she had become friends with the tom. Now she was sitting on that tall horse and looking around her, she wondered how much the man would be like Pip the cat.

Her eyes scanned the glade, taking it all in as Pip pulled the bucket out of the well. It was a large glade, veering down towards the well and entirely surrounded by trees. To her left, there was an incline and the trees grew thick and old, their roots twisting out the ground to support their seemingly gravity-defying growth. To her right, the trees seemed more friendly and spread out, their trunks reaching tall and strong. Up the hill were two buildings she had not taken in before, one of which must have been the house she had woken up in.

"Did you build all of this?" Amys asked gesturing to the well and to the buildings at the top of the hill, while also attempting to get off the horse.

"You really are full of questions, aren't you? No, I didn't - it was like this when I came here. All I did was patch a few things up," he sighed pulling the now full bucket to the edge of the well and balancing it there.

Then in a few quick strides he was at Izzy's side and he lifted her down from the horse. Once she was down, she ran jumping and skipping around the well, basking in the smell of fresh grass and the warmth of the sunlight. Pip looked on, holding Izzy's reins. When Amys looked at him every so often, he seemed like he was in deep and intense conversation with the black mare.

SNAP!

All three of them looked up at the forest line to see a quick movement, like something was running away from them. Pip grabbed the crossbow attached to Izzy's saddle and told her to stay as he carefully loaded a bolt and started stalking forward. Amys didn't really know what to do with herself apart from to keep following him, attempting to mimic his precise movements with her untrained feet.

He noiselessly moved into the forest. Amys even stood still a few times to listen and all she could hear was the sounds of birds distantly chirping their merry song in the forest. Sometimes he, too, would stop, if only to listen to the air for a moment and then continue moving with the same silent movements. He always kept his crossbow close to his chest, but it was aimed at the floor. Amys had a feeling that if whatever had made that sound came, he would be more than ready for it.

After some time, Pip fell on his chest on a mound of earth, levelling his crossbow on the mound. He kept his eyes pinned on looking down the bolt, even when she moved to join him, copying his position of laying on his front. She opened her mouth to say something, but he put his finger to his lips and her questions remained unformed in her mouth. He then moved his finger to point forward and her eyes followed the finger to see a deer standing still in the forest nibbling at a patch of grass. Her eyes fixed on it, wide and surprised, but before she could say anything more, she heard a thsssssp sound…. and suddenly the deer fell.

She looked to her side and Pip was already standing up, placing the crossbow around his shoulders. As he jumped over the mound, Amys looked on at the deer, her eyes welling up with tears ready to overflow, but she didn't want to cry. Her father had once explained to her where the meat they ate come from, and although she didn't much like the thought of it, she didn't expected to see it happen in front of her. But maybe if he could do this to a deer, he could maybe do that to THEM.

"Can you do that to people? With the crossbow?" asked Amys, with every word becoming more confident that she would not cry.

"Sometimes. Why would a little girl want to know about that?" asked Pip.

He hoisted the deer onto his shoulders to take home. They would at least eat well that night.

"That's the reason I told Father and everyone else we should come here. So, someone can do that to the masked men," she explained with little cracks in her voice as she pointed to the bolt coming from the body of the deer.

Pip looked at her in deep thought for a moment and then looked to the dead body of the deer on his shoulders.

"I think we should go home now," he said, and without a word took her hand and walked back through the forest towards Izzy, a grim expression on his face.

# CHAPTER 4

## THE SLEEPLESS NIGHT

*T*ristan had asked his grandparents if he could sleep in the barn for his last night at the farm. Of course, they had agreed. He doubted they would refuse him anything that evening, and now he was lying on his back in the hay loft. There was a window up there in the hay loft that had no pane and so he had a perfect view of the night's sky. His grandfather used to tell him the stories of great heroes and heroines long dead that made up the night's sky, although his grandfather claimed they were immortal. His favourite story was always of The Warrior, and he repeated it to himself now, as he felt no desire to sleep. There was something about the legendary soldier and all his daring feats that made him hope that one day he'd be able to do something like it. Maybe not take on a whole army, but something at least a little heroic.

He turned onto his side to get a proper view of the sky. In doing so, he allowed the warm night air to blow gently onto his face. The next day he would be away from Tindale and on his way to be a soldier for the King. He didn't really mind who he was fighting for as long as he got all the glory of being a hero. He probably would miss the farm and the village, and especially his grandparents; after all, it was all he had known.

As his mind wondered about the people and the things he might miss about the place, he suddenly remembered. Isabella. He had been so taken up with becoming a hero and fighting that he forgot about his best friend, his friend since before he could remember. He quickly, and as silently as he could, stood up in the hay loft, knowing that he had to say goodbye to her.

His grandfather had always described the footsteps of his grandson as resembling a stampede of elephants, so he was rather proud of the lack of noise he made as he slid down the ladders.

Tristan landed rather haphazardly at the bottom of the barn. The earthen floor was covered in a dusting of hay and it reeked with the smell of farm animals. He ran as quickly as he dared to the back of the barn and slipped out the back door and into the warm humid night. He knew the farm like the back of his hand, but he equally didn't want to wake his grandparents for any reason. He knew they already worried enough about most things, so he didn't want to add intruders to that list.

In a sort of crouch jog, Tristan moved swiftly around to the back of the farmhouse, attempting to keep at least a small piece of cover between him and his grandparent's bedroom window on the ground floor. This did involve sometimes having to roll from the tree to the plough, and even crawl on his elbows underneath the cart. He considered it all good practice for any sneaking behind enemy lines they might ask him to do.

Just as he saw his usual route to the Harper's farm, he stepped forward with a little too much confidence.

SNAP!

The stick underneath his foot broke into two pieces, sickeningly loud in the silence of the night. He froze completely still, feeling the hairs on his arms stand upright to attention. His back was to the farmhouse so he wouldn't know whether his grandparents were even stirring. He stood transfixed on the spot hoping beyond hope that all the jokes he had made about them being hard of hearing were true.

After what seemed to him to be an eternity, he decided if he was going to be caught, it would have already happened. He gingerly took his foot off the stick and breathed a sigh of relief. A sigh that he feared again was a little too loud. He quickly looked over his shoulder to see if it had been the straw to break the camel's back. But everything seemed as silent as before, so he let himself swallow his fear and he ran into the woods. As the wind below into his face and the night's air poured into his lungs, he realised that he didn't know what an elephant or camel looked like, but he smiled to himself not supposing it mattered much; he doubted he would ever see either one of them.

The route he would normally have taken, would have taken him directly to Isabella's family farm. A scamper through the woods, through the abandoned farmhouse and straight past the large pond, over a few fences and he'd be there. But couple of years previously, the McArthurs had moved into the abandoned farmhouse, and so he now had to take the longer route via a few country lanes. Not that he didn't like the couple. His grandparents said they were very lovely. It's just that he felt he needed more time to pluck up the courage to talk to someone who regularly carried a sword and whose wife was from Malancore. Not that there was anything wrong with either; he himself would have loved to carry around a sword and Rosa seemed like a very lovely woman, but he still found them more than a little strange.

Yet this was not a night for being faint hearted and he also figured he may want to get back to the hay loft before sunrise when he and his grandfather were to head towards Tindale. He took a deep breath and set the pace of his feet towards the McArthur's farm. The dark of the night obscured most of Tristan's vision, but he didn't really need to see. He knew where he was going and he was sure he could probably navigate his way there with his eyes shut. Running all the way, soon the glow of lantern light came into his view. He slowed his run into a slow jog and crouch. The chances were that they were asleep in their bed, but he also didn't want their first conversation about him to be about him sneaking through their premises.

He slowed all the way down as he got to the stone wall that marked the boundary of the farmhouse. The wall itself ran along a dirt road that joined a larger lane that connected all the farms east of Tindale and ran straight to the newly repaired farmhouse. Tristan peaked over the wall to see if the coast was clear for a quick vault and a sprint over a few fences and directly into the Harper's farm. To his dismay, the moonlight revealed two figures standing at the edge of the large pond, the white reflections bouncing off the water and illuminating the ghost-like couple.

Tristan quickly ducked back behind the wall. He didn't believe in ghosts or any sort of magic or superstition, and so he wasn't scared of the way they appeared. But he was terrified of being caught by them. The people of both Pickland and Malancore had very similar reputations in Valander and that was regarding their volatile tempers. He certainly didn't want to be on the receiving end of either one. But despite his fears, he knew he had to at least say goodbye to his friend.

Summoning his courage, he jumped over the wall and ran across the road and over the wall at the other side. Once he was over, he sat stock still, listening out for any sound of alarm but all he could hear was his heavy breathing. He stood up slowly, keeping the couple at the side of the pond in view, again making sure there was always a tree between him and them. He moved as swiftly as he dared from tree to tree, knowing that he had to get closer to the pond in order to be able to confidently find his way to the Harper's farm.

As he got closer to them, he realised they were talking in almost whispers so that he couldn't hear them even if he tried, and admittedly he had tried. They seemed only absorbed in each other and in particular on Rosa's stomach for some reason. Maybe a midnight talk about stomach complaints was a part of their strange culture...

He saw Joshua look down one more time at Rosa's stomach and then they embraced, so he didn't wait for another opportunity. He moved forward from tree to tree in the crouch jog that he had used earlier, and round the pond. By the time he got the fence separating the McArthur's farm-house from the Harper's land, he checked over his shoulder one last time to see if he had been noticed. The embrace was still not over, and Tristan realised he could have got away with a casual walk through the trees, but he also knew he would never have risked it. After that last look, he leapt over the sturdy wooden fence and ran towards the home strait.

When he eventually got to the Harper's farm, the stitch in his side was reminding him why he shouldn't have had a second helping of his grandmother's stew. But he was there and not in bad time either. Now the next thing to do was wake up Isabella without arousing her parents or her younger sister. They had snuck out into the night many times over the years for things like midnight feasts and to see fireflies, but now her younger sister had moved into her room from her parent's, things were a little more dangerous. He still decided the usual signal would work for the occasion.

He picked up a stone from the ground outside the farm-house, not big enough that it would smash the glass but equally not too small that it would get caught on the breeze. He threw it at her window. When he was younger, he would have to find a few stones because he would inevitably miss the first few, but now he had it down to a fine art and it hit the glass perfectly making the satisfying sound it should. He then stepped back and made three owl calls, again something he had had to practice when they had agreed on this code. But now he thought he was good at it. Then all he could do was wait, and hope that he wouldn't have to redo the entire process again.

It wasn't long before her face came to the window, her hands either side of it, her eyes scanning the ground. They brightened up as soon as they saw him. Tristan immediately went to the side of the house and grabbed a ladder, and after some struggle, he placed it against the side of the house so that its end balanced against the windowsill. He then turned his back while sitting on the ladder, hearing the sound of her window being opened and someone getting onto the ladders. Isabella wore night dresses and so she had a developed a way that he could support the ladder while also making sure he didn't see anything he shouldn't. He personally didn't think they needed to, as dresses were usually good at covering up people, but every time he had suggested they didn't need it, she had thumped him on the arm.

When he could hear her getting closer to the bottom of the ladder, he stepped forward sufficiently for her to descend the full way. He then turned to see his best friend standing there before him, and he couldn't help but smile. They used to be very similar in height when they were younger, in fact, she had always been a little taller than him and she would always let him know that. But then he had shot up in height and now he was the taller one. She had grown a little taller

31

too, but not enough to make up the difference. She had light brown hair, which ran long down her back, her eyes were bright and she always had the best ideas. Tristan did believe that she was very pretty, but he'd never tell her that. It wasn't really something you'd tell your best friend.

"What are you grinning at Tris?" she said in a condescending tone, but with a smile on her face.

He was convinced she had learned the voice from her mother, but at least when she said it, she meant it in fun; he wasn't so sure with Grace Harper so he usually avoided her.

"I'm just happy to see you Izz," he replied,

His grin was becoming wider - it was always good to see her.

"It's quite late, Tris."

"I couldn't sleep."

"Good, me neither. Let's go see if my dad still has some apples in the barn."

And with that, she walked towards the barn. That was partly why he liked her so much; she was always ready for an adventure and always had the best way to go about doing it. He followed after her towards the Harpers large barn, just looking forward to being with her.

The Harpers were the richest farmers around Tindale mainly due to Herbert Harper's apple cider that merchants passing through would always buy. That meant their barn was the largest in the area and therefore also had the most hiding places. He knew the barn well. He was there when it was first built by as many men that Herbert could hire, and the two friends had spent many a happy time playing hide and seek there or making forts out of broken barrels.

Isabella led them to one of their favourite spots, coincidently next to a barrel that always had a gap just large enough for an apple to fit through. This hole was often use of by Izz, but her dad never noticed and neither of them were going to breath a word about it. She struck a match against a barrel and lit a lantern that was hanging off a beam, revealing their usual spot. Izz leapt to first her usual position on top of a pile of bags of oats, immediately selecting an apple from those available, and he stood before her leaning on one of the stacked up barrels, letting himself remember all of these details. Especially Isabella.

"What are you looking at?" she asked taking a hefty bite into the apple and letting the juice run down her chin.

"You know, just trying to remember the details. Like how silly you look right now," laughed Tristan, and without missing a beat, Isabella threw her apple directly at him.

She was always good at throwing, and it hit him directly in the side of the head. They both laughed together, both now with juice on their faces.

Tristan then took his traditional place next to her pile, leaning against the wooden wall with his feet up against a support beam. They ate, talked and laughed like they usually did, with Izz handing him an apple every time he wanted one and he took her cores and threw them across the barn. They usually picked a target so Tristan could prove that he was getting better at throwing things, but for some reason that night they didn't really feel like it so the apple cores hit off various barrels and tools for making the cider, exploding into shards of apple, making them both burst into laughter and general fits of giggling. Perhaps they were more grown up now, but he felt like he could have fun with Izz.

"Do you remember when you tried to steal Mr Grainger's chicken?" laughed Isabella handing Tristan another apple core.

"Well, you told me you wanted it for a pet - how was I to know it was his prize chicken?" laughed Tristan taking it and throwing it as far as he could into the dark barn, and a second later heard the satisfying noise of it exploding.

"How was I supposed to know he kept five dogs?" laughed Isabella in an attempt at mimicking his voice.

"We ran all the way into the forest because of those stupid dogs."

"You didn't even get the chicken!" pointed out Izz making herself giggle so hard she fell onto his arm; he laughed a little too.

He could still remember just how terrified he was when they were running into the woods, but Izz seemed to enjoy every moment. That was the kind of courage that he needed to be a hero.

"I didn't get the chicken. But we did end up finding the waterfall. I would argue that was better than a chicken," observed Tristan letting Isabella's head move up on his shoulder, and he looked down her and smiled.

"It was better than a chicken."

"That is, until you got too chicken to go there anymore."

This time Tristan made himself laugh, but he quickly stopped after she shot him a glare.

"You know exactly why I couldn't do it anymore, and it wasn't because I was scared. You know it was my mother who said it was indecent for a young lady to be jumping into a waterfall in nothing but my skin, especially with you," she said and she strained the last two words for a reason, Tristan didn't know why.

"Yeah I know. But you were always the bravest. You never seemed to be scared, no matter how high you got up the waterfall, you'd never hesitate to jump in," he smiled, looking down at her with bright eyes, hoping to avoid her being annoyed at him for too long.

"You'd always dance around like a headless chicken before you jumped in, you were so scared you were going hit something or miss the water, or whatever," she added.

She looked back up at him, adjusting her position on his shoulder.

"That's very true, I was very scared," he agreed, looking forward and remembering the fear that always shot up his back as visions of him landing wrong had gone through his head. That would not be him now; he would be a glorious hero.

"Are you scared?"

"Well I haven't been there in a while so I'm not sure."

"No silly, of everything that happened today. The going to war and all that. My dad seems very scared by it, he can't stop hugging my mother and she can't stop crying. But you don't seem as bothered as they are," Isabella observed her bright eyes shining up at him.

The best he could do was look forward. He hadn't really noticed that Herbert had been there in the church with him, but now he thought about it he did remember him sweating like all the other men apart from him. And maybe Joshua.

"I don't feel scared really at all. I've been scared of a lot of things in my life, the waterfall, Mr Grainger's dogs, but I did them anyway, but this feels different. I really want to do what the heroes in stories do and go out find glory," he declared.

He leapt to his feet in front of her, knowing every word he said to her was true.

"Well - by the look of it you have enough fool hardiness within you to go between you, my dad and all the men in the village," she commented.

She followed him to her feet and stood looking up at him, her sun-beam eyes staring up.

"I will miss you Izz, you know that, right?" he reassured to her looking down at her beautiful eyes, and face and everything else.

"Just make sure this isn't goodbye. You take your courage

and you come back in one piece and bring my dad back too while you're at it," she said and she gave him a hug. He hugged her back and seized her tight, not really wanting to let her go.

Her hair got in his face, but he didn't really mind, he liked hugging her. It felt…. nice. Like home.

"I promise I'll come back Izz."

"You better, or I'll kill you," she threatened marching towards the barn door.

He had to speed up to catch up with her and when he did, they walked at a slow pace towards the ladder still propped up. On their way he told her what he had seen at the McArthur's arm and told her his theory that it must be a strange custom for curing stomach ache, and all she did was laugh and tell him he was an idiot. They got a lot slower just before the ladder and stood in front of it for a while talking about this and that, about nothing in particular, both of them just wanting a reason to linger. The conversation did eventually reach a lull and they stood for a moment just looking at each other.

"Well, I guess this is goodbye," she said looking back up the ladder to her window.

"I guess it is," he replied not taking his eyes off her for a second.

"Before you go take this," she said undoing her necklace and handing it to him.

The chain was a simple silver, but hanging from it was a beautifully made oakleaf. He stared at it in his hand.

"But Izz…"

"No buts Tristan. It's just a reminder to come back."

She then reached up and kissed his cheek and before he could react, she started her ascent up the ladder. For a moment Tristan stood in shock looking up at her, his cheek burning. He only snapped out of it when he saw her give him one last wave, and the window shut. He stood for a moment, just looking at the oakleaf on the necklace; the way it shone so brightly really did remind him of her eyes. It had been her favourite necklace, and he swore to himself he'd bring it back in one piece, as well as himself and her father. For the sake of Isabella, he would.

He moved the ladder a little slower that night. The walk home was a little longer. He didn't really want the night to end, but he did know that it would have to end eventually, and he would have to be in the hay loft before it did. His cheek burned all the way home, but he was sure it was because he was cold.

As he got back to the farmhouse and slipped back into the barn, all he could think about was Isabella and the kiss on his cheek.

# CHAPTER 5

## FIRELIGHT

*P*eter looked down at Amys as she slept, and smiled to himself. Just the night before he'd held her in his arms and thought it would be for the last time, and now here he was looking down at her sleeping softly. How grateful he felt. Never before had he been so close to death. He had felt like dying after Sarah had passed away, but the other night their imminent death was not just a feeling. But here he was sitting in a warm room, watching over his daughter as she slept, and it was all thanks to the man they had tried to find. Only he found them.

His eyes always returned to Amys and the smile that still remained on her lips. She had had an exciting day by the sounds of it but he had missed most of it. He had woken to the sounds of the door opening and Amys running to his side and excitedly telling him everything she had done. He had barely had time to take in his surrounding and process the events of the night before. He then sat at the table with Amys on his lap as she explained everything that had happened, often jumping from the beginning to the end and then somewhere in the middle, and then back the beginning, as she remembered details. He had listened most attentively, but he was drawn to look at the man she called Pip.

He was a grim man with a face set in a stern expression, his eyes dark and giving away absolutely nothing. Peter was used to studying other people. It helped with bargaining at the shop, but attempting to read Pip was like trying to read a blank piece of paper. He did notice various scars on the man's hands and a rather impressive wound that ran down his neck that had gone white with time. He was surprised that a man like this had time for an insistent little girl like his Amys, but he seemed to tolerate her presence, and if Peter didn't know any better, he'd say that Pip actually liked her company.

Pip had brought a dead deer inside with him. Amys had explained that he had shot the deer himself with his crossbow and proceeded to explain her feelings on the matter. She explained that she had been scared at first, but then she realised that he could do the same thing to the masked men, so she didn't feel as bad. Goodness – how he hoped that Pip could. As she was telling this story, Pip had walked out, grim faced as usual, taking the deer with him. After some time, he came back and began making them a stew from the meat from the beast.

To Peter, the stew smelt heavenly and it tasted truly divine, and it was this stew smell that lingered as he gave Amys one last kiss on the forehead and drew the curtain between the bed and the rest of the room. He turned to see Pip gazing into the fire, the same grim expression on his face as he carved away at a stick with a carving knife. Peter took a seat at the table trying not to disturb the man who had already helped them so much.

"Is she asleep?" Pip asked, still looking into the fire.

His voice was as stern and level as his face, and it sent chills down Peter's back.

"Yes, she is. She had a good day by the sounds of it, and I suppose a very eventful night too. She'll sleep well tonight."

He tried to keep his voice level as his eyes were glued to the figure sitting in front of the fire. The greying man nodded and looked into the fire a little longer, before standing up and turning his chair to face Peter. Now that the fire was behind him and the shadows danced around him, he seemed even more forbidding. Peter couldn't help but swallow as his eyes fixed on the man. For someone who didn't talk much or dress with extravagance, the man seemed to take up the entire room just by his presence.

"Quite the eventful night," he almost whispered looking at Peter directly and then quickly to the floor, as if he had just remembered something.

"I think you're probably owed many explanations. You must be thinking I am such a terrible father bringing his daughter into a wood that the stories say are haunted and full of monsters," started Peter trying to remember to speak at a normal speed and not waffle too much. Sarah had always said if he could take the longest way round a story, he would and also take every alleyway and side street, so it was very important he focused on not doing that.

"I'm not particularly one to judge," replied Pip he said with the same level voice as he looked up from the floor and stared straight into Peter's soul, "But the wolves are running and that hasn't happened since I was a young man. So you'd better have a really good reason why you were apparently trying to find me,"

"Well - where should I start?" stuttered Peter trying to get his head together and his rather bendy story straight.

"I think most people start at the beginning," Pip stated opening his legs and leaning his arms on them, shifting eyes between the floor, Peter, and the roof in regular shifts, but Peter knew that he was listening with every fibre.

"Well... I run a supply shop in Little Carr, a town stead not far from here. Sorry maybe that's too far into the beginning," Peter said stopping himself and closed his eyes, visualising how he should tell the tale. Pip just continued his lean forward, his back arched and eyes alive.

"It started one day when some strange men in masks rode into the village," Peter started, and immediately Pip stopped his routine looking up and down to stare him directly in the eye, or maybe it wasn't him; it seemed like it could be something behind him.

"What kind of masks?"

"They covered their faces. Sorry, all I remember from them is carrying various weapons and wearing these white masks," replied Peter not exactly knowing what Pip wanted to hear, but the talks of masks seemed to interest him and it gave Peter growing confidence in what he had to say.

"White masks. Are you sure?"

"Yes, they were white. They looked almost porcelain, covering the upper half of their faces," replied Peter squinting as he attempted to recall the memory.

Pip looked very sternly at the floor, his eyes like shadows because of the light behind him. After a couple of moments, he gestured for him to continue the story.

"Ah yes. Well, they rode in on horseback and with weapons and told us to bring them all the gold that we had. Their leader didn't carry a weapon and when a few people tried to resist, he waved his hand in the air and turned the entire sky around us black. After that people were so scared, they gave all they had and more."

"Turned the sky black," repeated Pip looking to Peter but in a more inquisitive way, his eyebrow arched while his head turned to one side.

"I wouldn't have believed it either, but I saw it with my own eyes. The sky went as black as night, probably darker.

And from then on, they've been camping near the village robbing travellers and coming in for food, supplies or just about anything that takes their fancy," continued Peter noting Pip's deep interest in the events that took place.

"This is probably where I come in," Pip observed getting to his feet and forcing a smile in Peter's direction.

"It's been ten days. We hardly have anything left. So, we had a meeting, the entire village in my good friend's Jacklin's tavern because we had to do something," said Peter turning in his seat as Pip walked over to the fireplace and stared into the flames.

Silent and pondering, his eyes still as dark as they were when he was sat in front of the blaze.

"It was Amys' idea to find you."

"She said something to me along those lines."

"Normally children aren't allowed at those kinds of meetings, but no-one felt safe leaving anyone at their homes. When she suggested the idea of trying to find the warrior that merchants claimed lived in Malcoren, none of us thought it was a particularly good idea. It just happened to be the best one."

Peter looked up at the person he had risked so much to find, hoping to see how much he could try to read from his face.

"Those other ideas must have been pretty bad," chuckled Pip looking up from the fire and turning back to Peter, the flickering shadows dancing behind him.

"And I was the only one who had a horse that wasn't stolen by the masked men, so I volunteered to go and Amys wouldn't let me go alone," continued Peter, "She said she didn't want to live without a mother or a father, or words to those effect."

"Well, that would do it," Pip said looking towards where Amys was sleeping and looked to the floor again.

"We had to leave at night because we didn't want 'them' to see us leaving. And that's about everything really. I think you know the rest of the story," Peter finished not wanting to go over the wolves and the events of the night before.

"I suppose I do know the rest," Pip said detached voice, his eyes on the floor, avoiding the other man's gaze.

"You certainly have seem to have the skills that are needed to deal with this kind of thing. You made short work of those wolves and you seem very handy with a crossbow. Please, Pip, please. We will give you all that we have, although it's not much, everything that we can put together is yours," begged Peter temporarily forgetting his fear of the other man, instead thinking about what would happen if he couldn't get Pip to come with him.

There was silence as Peter looked intently at the man opposite him, deep in thought. All that could be heard was the crackle of flames and the only movement was the dancing of light on the shadows.

"I'll help you," Pip said breaking the silence.

Peter stood to his feet in jubilation almost shouting for joy, but he stopped himself when he remembered Amys sleeping in the bed. Pip still stared grimly at the floor. He shook off whatever thought held him captive and looked up right towards Peter. Peter noted that his eyes were a dark shade of brown, and full of intent.

"Thank you, we will give you whatever you ask of us."

"I'm doing it for nothing. Consider it a favour for a friend," promised Pip, and Peter had a feeling that he wasn't the friend that Pip had in mind. As he said this, Pip opened a cupboard, taking out various assortments of weapons and placing them onto the table. Laying them out, he simply stared at them a while.

"You should get some sleep, Peter; we leave at first light," said the greying warrior not looking up from the weapons, an array of four swords of different lengths, many daggers, a throwing axe and a tow-headed battle axe. Peter did feel very tired even though that he had spent a large portion of the day sleeping.

Giving Pip a nod, Peter wasn't sure whether the warrior had seen him slip away off to bed. He lay next to his daughter and she moved in her sleep so that she could be close to his chest. Peter felt something he hadn't felt in a long time - hope. Still, he felt like there was something about Pip that he couldn't quite put his finger on. But what did that matter when Pip had said yes to him. That answer was worth its weight in gold.

Sleep took over Peter quickly, so he didn't hear the small sounds Pip made walking around the house to various corners and nooks. He had had to be silent so many times that he walked quietly around the house without even thinking about it. The last location that Pip visited was a small chest underneath the bed. The father and daughter slept so soundly that they didn't notice it being opened and the contents being taking out gently. And as the night wore on and the fire slowly died, the shadows swallowed all the empty places now in the home.

He wasn't planning on coming back, whatever happened next.

# CHAPTER 6

## GOODBYES

The sun was beginning to rise when Tristan and his grandfather saw the buildings that made up the village of Tindale. If his mind hadn't been on other things, Tristan would have admired the beautiful summer morning sky with its elegant mix of reds and oranges, shaped to look like a canvas. Yet from the moment that his grandfather had shaken him awake in the wee hours of the morning to the moment that Tindale came into view, his mind was a cacophony of thoughts and images ranging from how he would learn to use a sword - heroes always wielded swords in the stories - to the memories of last night. It was all whirling round his head driven by excitement to start on his journey.

His grandfather walked next to him with a very set face. He hadn't said much to him after the initial waking up. Tristan guessed he was likely tired. His grandfather was used to early mornings, but he wasn't getting any younger and his grandmother constantly reminded him he wasn't a young man anymore, and should take on more help at the farm than simply Tristan, but his grandfather had always dismissed these ideas. His eyes looked like they were damp and red. When Tristan had asked why they were like that, he replied something about a condition that comes with old age and kept on in silence. Tristan knew that he was going to miss his grandparents very much, and Isabella, and the farm. But he also knew that he needed to go and he would have chosen to go even if he had been given the choice to stay.

They were close to the entry of Tindale when his grandfather stopped for a moment, still looking forward to the path. Tristan stopped with him, looking at him closely, aware the sergeant with the large nose had told them to be there by sun rise. After a moment, his grandfather looked directly at him and gave a forced smile.

"Well Tris - you've become quite the young man; you look the spitting image of your father," said his grandfather choking over the few words.

When Tristan moved closer to see if he was all right, he simply put out his hand to stop him and coughed into a handkerchief for a moment.

"Your grandmother and I realise that you might not be back for some time, so we wanted you to have this. It was your father's," he said.

He took off his rucksack and taking out a long dagger, presented it to Tristan. Tristan took it and unsheathed it, looking at the blade in every detail and in total awe.

"It may not be a lot of use in all these big wars that you might get caught up in, but it might just bring you back to you grandmother and I," he choked again, and this time didn't even pretend not to be crying, his tears flowing down his withered old cheeks.

Tristan quickly sheathed the dagger and embraced his grandfather, he himself with tears rolling down his face freely.

"I'm coming back, I promise," he vowed holding close the man who had raised him.

They stayed like that a moment, until his grandfather let him go, mentioning something about being late as he brushed away the rest of his tears with his kerchief. Tristan smiled and helped his grandfather get his rucksack back up onto his back.

Their walk into Tindale from there was a little slower than the pace that they had set before. Tristan didn't think either of them wanted to hurry more than necessary. They got to the tall oak tree that had stood in the middle of the village since its beginnings in the early forming of the King-doms. It stood proud and strong, very unlike the huddle of men and their families that were standing under it. Each of them held onto their wives and children, saying tender words, promising they wouldn't be gone long and they'd bring them back something from the capital. They tried to wear strong faces, like those men from stories who went to fight for the King gladly, but their eyes told a very different story. Each man also carried various sorts of farming tools that could be considered a weapon: wood axes, mallets and one man even had a pitchfork. Not exactly the weapons of soldiers.

As Tristan and his grandfather took their places under the tree, he saw the Harpers out of the corner of his eye. Herbert looked truly miserable as he dragged his axe behind him, being led by his wife to the tree as she talked about this and that, about how he needed to find certain things for her in the capital when they got there. Isabella and Claire walked behind them, and she smiled back to him when their eyes met for a moment.

There were men there that Tristan had been scared of when he was growing up, men that he had witnessed grow bellies and greying hair with the passing of years. It was very strange to see them all now on the brink of leaving for war. It made him shiver but he told himself that was due to the fresh morning breeze that rustled the leaves of the large oak tree.

Just then the sergeant and his four knights rode on horseback with great speed into the centre of the village. He thought they had bunked at the mayor's house and so everyone expected them to come from that direction, but they rode in from the East road, the one they were likely going to head towards. Tristan guessed that they had been looking for something or making sure the road was good enough for travelling, but going by the scarlet of the sergeant's face, it had not gone well.

"I'm glad to see most of you made it. That is some good news at least, much better than these troublesome bandits we were chasing all night," he vented, turning his horse to the side as the other four soldiers spread out across the square, giving their horses some rest.

"We'll make soldiers of some of you," continued the Sergeant, his eyes scanning over the sorry bunch of men, making Tristan wonder what would happen to those who didn't get made into soldiers.

The sergeant's eye stopped when he got to Joshua and his focus was on the sword he carried.

"You there, you're very young to be carrying a weapon like that, especially in a place like this. Where did you get it?" his voice screeched as he raised it, as his finger pointed more towards the weapon than the man.

"I served in the Dragonborn conquest, in Malancore," Joshua replied, his Pickish accent was as hard as steel and made the other men around him wince.

"Can you use it?"

"As well as any man who survived the dragon fire," Joshua responded, and Tristan noticed his hand reaching for the hilt of the weapon, his grip loosely around it, his other arm still around his wife. Tristan supposed dragon fire must have been a metaphor of some kind, but it still made many of the men around him stare at him and then to one another.

"We at least have one soldier in this sorry bunch," muttered the sergeant under his breath as he turned his horse again towards the road.

"Say your last goodbyes now. I plan on making good time today and we're late already. We will be meeting many of the other new recruits at the Bradley Manor camp not one day's march from here. From there we will make our way to the capital and to war!" shrieked the sergeant.

He then rode towards two of the other soldiers on horseback, and as everyone said their goodbyes, Tristan saw him point to the tree and say, "That will do for those who tried to escape service of the King."

With that, the two of them rode away out of the village, again at a speed that Tristan had never witnessed before this day.

Tristan gave his grandfather one last short hug, neither of them wanting to show too much public display of affection in case the tears started again. They then stood as everyone else said their goodbyes. Every so often his grandfather would ask him if he had a certain thing and Tristan would answer he did have it, but he didn't even check. It wouldn't matter if he didn't, there wouldn't be a whole lot he could do about it anyway.

"All right men – let's get moving!" screamed the Sergeant.

He motioned them to follow him down the road. Many men gave their wives one last hug, their children one last kiss on the head and then they picked up their weapon and moved forward.

"I'll come back, I promise," Tristan vowed, hoping his knees wouldn't give way underneath him.

"I know you will, lad," choked his grandfather, the tears starting again.

Rosa approached the two of them, in the gliding way that seemed to be normal for the people from Malancore.

"Don't worry about your grandfather, Tristan. I'll get him home safe and sound. Now you go and join the rest of the men," she promised, her voice like the songs of birds and her accent enunciating every letter in the word.

Tristan looked over his shoulder to see that most of the men had fallen in line behind the sergeant's steed. He gave one more glance to his grandfather now being held up by Rosa and rushed to fall in line with the other men, putting the long dagger into his belt.

The soldiers barked orders to the men, arranging them into lines of three, and through some shuffling and much shouting, they were finally ready to leave. The sergeant snapped his reins of his horse and moved forward at marching pace. All the other men followed suit attempting to keep pace with that of the walk of the horse in front of them. Many of these men weren't used to walking at such a brisk pace, but they feared the soldiers more than they did losing their breath or developing a stitch in their sides, so they tried to keep up.

Tristan was near the back, so he got one last opportunity to look back before he had to start walking. His grandfather was being held up by Rosa with one arm, but with the other he waved his cherkief and forced a smile. His eye moved to see Isabella waving her father off. Once again their eyes met and she stopped for a moment to smile, and he, there and then, knew he needed to keep his promise and come back to Tindale. As he turned to start walking, he noticed he wasn't the only person looking back. Joshua, too, finally turned his face towards the road, a single tear drop rolling down one of his cheeks. Tristan tried to find the energy to smile, but

instead he set his feet to walking and his head to the motivation he had first experienced for going to war. When he
returned, he would have many stories of his heroic deeds to
tell.

They walked at the same pace for miles, many more miles
than Tristan had ever walked from home and he was excited
by every detail of the new terrain. Every tree and field looked
like had its own place in a story, maybe in his story. But these
were fleeting images as they relentlessly marched on. One
thing the stories didn't mention was how much marching the
soldiers had to do, or at least when they did, the tales would
describe the marching songs that roused the men's spirits.
But, as each mile went past and the heat of the summer
increased, the men just seemed to be more miserable, not
exactly in the mood for singing.

The sergeant rode at the front of the men, pulling down
his chainmail hood revealing his bald head which became
very red over the course of the morning. The other two
soldiers took it in turns to either ride behind the group or
ride before them and then come back after around ten
minutes, whisper something to the sergeant, and then ride
the other way. Tristan considered this was likely for a very
important reason as the men always looked very stern. But
maybe it was because the heat of the sun was constantly
beating on their faces. It was bad enough for those not in
armour, but he imagined it would be torture for the soldiers.

When the sun rose to its zenith, they arrived at a river
and the sergeant called a stop and the men halted with a
large collective sigh of relief. The sergeant turned his horse
to look down his large nose at them all. The only one of them
who didn't seem to be panting and sweating profusely was
Joshua, his shirt barely marked with sweat. Even the soldiers
on the horses looked relieved to be stopping.

"We will rest here for an hour or so until the sun is past

its highest point. I advise you fill your canteens at the river and use the trees for cover from the sun. We should be at the manor before nightfall, but I would recommend you recover your energy as much as you can; it's still many miles to go yet," he said.

His usual high-pitch tones failed to bother Tristan's ears so much; he was just relieved that they could stop the walking. All men practically rushed out of the ranks to refill their water and get some shade and rest. Tristan was among the last to refill his canteen, but he didn't mind; it gave him time to splash some water onto his face and clear his brow. It cooled him down and he already felt more energised. He joined the rough semi-circle the men had made in the shade, as every man pulled out the food that his wife had given him for lunch, the last time in a while that they would taste it.

Although the general mood of the men was not of comrades going off to war, this didn't stop them from being a little jolly together. Each man shared what he had with the others, and they even cracked a joke or two. Tristan's main focus was on food, so he didn't follow the conversation that was happening around him, but he did remember to laugh when everyone else did and mind his Ps and Qs. His grandmother had packed him a hearty meal with bread, some cheese, a couple of apples and an assortment of dried meats, small enough to carry but large enough to fill up a hungry man. He quickly traded away the apples and most of the bread and meat with some of the other men's food.

Mr Harper had some of his wife's apple pie. Most of the men there were scared of his wife, but none could deny her ability to make an exemplary apple pie. So, it was in high demand, and Tristan was fortunate enough to gain a piece. Mr Sinclair had brought a collection of meat pies which he was making a business of trading with the other men for steep favours when they eventually got to camp, all of course in fun. When Tristan enquired after one, Mr Sinclair simply gave it to him and gave a friendly smile; no cost required. The other men, too, had a range of food. Each shared what they had; he even got to try what Rosa had made for Joshua, a sort of pasty with meat in it. The taste was unusual to him, but it was filling and good.

When they had all stopped eating to relax, the mood was almost jovial. Some men started lighting pipes, and one of the soldiers even came over to offer some of his tobacco to the older men. Tristan happily lay with his rucksack behind his head, his eyes scanning the water and letting the breeze blow and cool off his face. This was worth all the marching.

The mood changed quickly when the other two soldiers rode into the camp and straight to the sergeant, grim expressions on their faces. The other men from Tindale stopped their chatter and jokes, their faces falling to match those of the soldiers. Tristan guessed that something had happened but, he didn't know what, just that it couldn't be good.

They weren't left to wallow in this shift in mood for long as the sergeant got on his horse and ordered the men back into file. They obeyed slowly and quietly, their eyes looking down rather than at the soldiers that flanked them. Their pace that afternoon was the same, but Tristan didn't remember as much as from the morning. It was a long blur of marching while looking at the ground, putting all his energy into not falling behind the pace. This seemed to be the practice of the other men as well, as they also kept their heads down and their rucksacks tight.

Tristan hardly noticed the light changing as the sun began its lazy descent, painting the sky once again. He did notice when they arrived at their camp because of what they saw when they marched over a hill. The Bradley family manor was a large building, built on a hill with a winding path that led to the door, the dark building ever hovering over them. It was made of dark stone and the clouds seemed to swirl around it, as if it was the eye of a forming tornado. It looked down upon a large valley which used to contain the Bradley family orchards, famous for their supply of various local fruits to the capital. Now it was full of tents of various shapes and sizes. Tristan had never seen so many people in one place and his mouth dropped open in amazement.

There were people all over starting to make fires; some had already made them and the air was filled with smoke that carried the smell of food to his nostrils. To his surprise, there weren't just men recruited for war in this camp; he even saw women and some children too, walking around the tents. They weren't usually mentioned in the stories of great armies, but he supposed there were things that would make more sense when he was properly in the camp.

He looked to the other Tindale men and they too were gazing down at unbelief, apart from Joshua who stood behind them hand on his sword, head turned to the left. Tristan gazed to follow his eyeline and nearly threw up in his mouth when he saw what Joshua had been gazing at. His involuntary reaction had startled some of the other men and soon they were all looking at the five men who hung from a large tree that hung over the valley. Tristan wanted to look away, but another part of him won't let him stop. His eyes locked at the horrific sight.

"Our host Lord Bradley and his sons. In case any of you think that not doing your duty to the Crown is an appealing idea," observed Sergeant Cleaver gazing over to the tree himself, his usual high-pitched voice uncharacteristically low.

"All right - that's enough staring for the evening. I, for one, want to get some warm food in me. When we get into the camp, you'll be assigned tents and a place to sleep. I recommend you get some rest; they may ask us to head for the capital in the morning and that's a hard march on no rest," he bellowed breaking the sober atmosphere.

Tristan couldn't imagine what the march to the capital would be like on no rest; the march today seemed to be bad enough to him. They marched slowly down into the valley taking the winding road that merchants would usually take when going via the manor to collect the fruits. Many of the trees ought to have been in full fruit, but most of the trees were bare, likely taken by the soldiers to supply food for the army. When they arrived in the valley, the sergeant rode off towards the manor and four soldiers guided them to the supply tent. They had to weave through many yellowing tents, not receiving so much as a glance from those who were already there. Newcomers to the camp must have been a fairly regular occurrence.

They were each given a sleeping mat, a blanket and a bowl. The soldiers divided them into rough groups of ten or eleven, and then pointed out to them the spot where they were supposed to set up camp for the night. Tristan trailed behind his group, part tired from the walk and part wanting to take in his surroundings.

Mr Sinclair, one of the villagers, took command of the group, giving instructions on how to put up the tent to some and telling others to get some firewood from the supply tents and get a fire going. Nobody had any energy left to complain, they simply nodded their heads and did what they were told to do. Soon enough the tent was up and they all had their rucksacks inside and bed rolls laid out, but more importantly the men had got a roaring fire going. They sat around the fire, eating the food they were given and warming what was left from lunch. Although each man was exhausted, they still sat and laughed with each other, and Tristan began to feel properly at ease with the men he remembered having to be respectful of when he was a lad.

The sky grew dark with a surprising suddenness, and soon all there that could be seen were the campfires that dotted the valley and the stars. All Tristan could see of the men were their faces and fronts revealed by the light of the fire, contented smiles on their faces, but in their eyes, they wished they could be seated before a fireplace rather than a campfire.

"Well, I hear rumour that we're going to be here at least three more days before we march to the capital. How does three days' rest do you lads? You look like you could do with some rest Tristan, although a young man like you would probably be used to staying up to all sorts of hours into the night," observed Mr Sinclair trying to involve Tristan in the campfire conversation.

"Well sir..." began Tristan.

"No sirs, not here lad. We're a long way from Tindale and we're going longer still. Just call me Harry or Harold, depending on which you prefer. But mind you, most people call me Harry, and the only person who calls me Harold is my missus when I'm in trouble," he laughed, and all the other men laughed with him.

"Well, erm, Harry. I won't mind sleeping for the next three days, if that's the case." Tristan replied, having to stop himself from saying sir again.

The other men nodded their agreements to his answer; Mr Harrison even raised his flask to the idea before he took another swig.

"Well lad, I imagine there's some reintroductions in order to avoid all the sirs and misters on the battle field, eh?" asserted Harry.

He reached over take a swig of something in a mug, and before Tristan could stop him, launched into the introductions.

"The one you would call Mr Harrison over there, the one who almost choked on his flask, his name is Frank."

That man raised his flask to him, his beard dripping the liquid in the flask.

"Over there you have Stephan, we call him Steve, and Jeffrey, we call him Jeff."

Harry pointed at two older men, their bellies large from good eating and greying hair from age.

"And, of course, you know the father of your sweetheart Isabella - Herbert."

With that the men laughed, and Tristan attempted to tell them that Isabella was just a good friend, but the men were too caught up in their own joke to listen. Even Herbert laughed, but Tristan was sure that his eyes screamed murder towards him.

"Lastly we have Joshua McArthur here."

Harry finished pointing towards Joshua, who simply let a small smile out towards Tristan, and Harry Sinclair shifted a little awkwardly with the embarrassment of introducing someone he'd hardly ever interacted with.

"You've really got this introduction thing down to a fine art, Harry, considering the young fellow you're making all the introductions to is a chicken thief," remarked James Grainger, the son of old man Grainger.

This statement nearly made Tristan leap out of his skin. He noted he had his father's thick eyebrows and scowl and he failed to notice the twinkle in his eyes. But soon it faded into a large smile, and it set everyone around the fire to laughing. Even Joshua cracked a smile. Apparently, the story of him running from old man Grainger's dogs wasn't just limited to him and Isabella.

"I jest, of course. I'm James, but most people call me Jamie - glad to meet you."

He chuckled to himself sitting next to Tristan extending a

hand. Tristan took it and they shook, and finally he felt the weight of that attempted theft fall off his shoulders.

The night wore on and the laughter faded into story-telling. Of course, Harold Sinclair told the most fantastical stories that made every lean in to listen closely to every word. Some of the others told some stories, but they'd always pass it back to him.

"…. And they all lived happily ever after," finished Harry with a flourish falling onto his rear end at the end.

His story had required, in his opinion, getting onto his feet for the full movement required to play four goblins that the hero had to sneak up on and take the princess back from.

"Harry, that story truly gets better every time you tell it," complimented Stephan throwing another piece of wood onto the fire and the sparks lit up into the air and floated up to meet the dark cloudless sky.

"Well - you've heard all my stories before. Joshua, we've never heard any of your stories, you fought in the Dragonborn invasion, so you must have picked up a few stories there, right?" inquired Harry looking to Joshua, and glancing for a moment at the sword he had at his side.

If Harry would have looked around the fire at the faces sitting there, as Tristan did, there were many strained looks in his direction, with eyes that warned caution.

"None of my stories are as entertaining as yours, I'm afraid," responded Joshua drinking deeply from his mug.

Any other person would have considered this the end of the conversation, but Harry thought otherwise.

"Come on, I for one would love to hear one. Maybe like how you ended up with a sword like that, right, lads?" entreated Harry.

He appealed to the group and in response the rest of the men murmured something that Harry took to be agreement. Joshua finished his mug and stood up in the firelight, drawing his sword in a swift movement. Tristan has never seen a sword like it before, or even really thought of swords like it; it was straight until it curved at the end. The steel was polished and flawless, its movements reflecting in the fire-light. He moved it back and forth, occasionally spinning it with a flourish to the amazement of the other men.

"I'm a soldier, at least I was a soldier. My father was a soldier in the campaign to take back the dark lands, and my grandfather fought in the wars to the north against the fire elves. So, you could say it's in my blood," he said balancing the sword in front of him for an impossible moment, and then back to the hum of swinging.

"I was with the Pickish garrison in Malancore when I was a little younger than Tristan here with my father and mother when the Dragonborn attacked the Port city of Rarecuseca. Of course, we moved in to aid in the defence of the city," he continued, his eyes reflecting the fire.

"All there was there was dragon fire and death. I happened to not die. For that the king saw fit to make me one of the royal guards. These are simply one of the swords the guard would carry," he said stopping the momentum of his sword and sliding it back into its sheath.

He sat back down each man staring at him in awe. Tristan let his mouth hang open. Joshua must have been just as young as he had been when he first went to war and he was a hero just like the stories. He hoped beyond anything that he would one day be able to have half as good as a story as that. But he also promised himself, he'd tell it better.

"So, there were Dragons. I thought that was just a story from the invasion," muttered James looking past Tristan to Joshua, with a mix of respect and fear in his years.

"Yes, there were. A lot of them. Many good men died to their breath," he responded grimly looking no one in the eye, just staring in the fire.

"You're a hero!" exclaimed Tristan under his breath.

But Joshua immediately turned his head to him in a quick motion and said, "No lad. In wars and battles, there's no heroes, just the dead and those who have to bury them."

Joshua's Pickish accent cut through each of the men. There was no easy reply to that and each of the men knew it, so they sat gazing into the fire light each to their own thoughts. They knew they were going to war, and Tristan couldn't help but wonder which one he'd be. After a few too many uncomfortable crackles of the fire, Harry got to his feet and stretched.

"Well - that was morbid. It's getting late. I'm going to sleep - see you in the morning lads," he said smiling at first, but quickly his face fell when he noticed the faces of the other men. He hurriedly stepped past Joshua and into the tent.

Slowly the other men trickled into the tent, not saying much to each other as they did apart from the occasional wish of good sleep. The fire soon turned to embers, but Tristan didn't feel like sleeping after what Joshua had said. After a some time, they were the only two sitting by the embers of the fire.

"You know what you said about no heroes and the burying the dead?" asked Tristan keeping his eyes on the embers.

"Yes. My apologies if I came off a little strong," Joshua replied also occupying himself with the dying fire. He looked as if he was going to add something to what he said, but he seemed to think better of it and kept his mouth closed.

"Will you promise me that I won't be the person to die?" said Tristan turning to look at Joshua, unaware he had let a tear roll down his cheek. He had made a promise he'd come back.

"I can't promise you that. I truly wish I could," he said

looking back at him with a sad smile, and Tristan saw something in the other man's eyes.

It wasn't fear or hate; it was pain. He looked away from him as soon as he could, his eyes returning to the embers.

"I can't promise you won't die, but what I will promise is, I will do everything in my power to get you home," he stated simply looking back to him, and Tristan knew that he meant every word he said.

"Well, I promise you the same thing then. I'll get you back to Rosa," vowed Tristan. At this, Joshua smiled briefly, staring to the sky for a moment.

He then held out his hand for Tristan, and he took it and shook it. In front of the dying flames they sealed their promise. Soon after with many yawns, Tristan went to bed, leaving Joshua to sit still gazing at the embers.

# CHAPTER 7

## HELP

*T*he sun rose slowly into the sky, shedding the light into Malcoren as three figures and a horse made their way through the trees. The forest was thick with trees that grew beyond sight when you stood at the bottom of them, their branches stretching out to catch as much light as they could. However, some rays of light managed to slip past the defence of the trees and bring a little brightness to the forest floor. The forest was considerably less intimating than the night when Peter had desperately ridden through it.

It did also help that Pip seemed to know the forest and its trails like the back of his hand. They had risen early, just as the sun was rising, and they had been walking ever since. Peter looked back to see Amys happily dozing on the neck of the large mare that Pip referred to as Izzy. She looked very content and that made Peter smile; a warmness grew in his heart every time he saw her happy. Pip had placed her on the horse as they left, but she wasn't the first thing he had placed on her. By the looks of it, he had been very busy that previous evening in preparation for leaving as Izzy carried many things wrapped in blankets and various small containers on her back. Peter was just grateful that there was still room for Amys in the midst of it all.

Pip himself walked in front of them, his crossbow in his hand and his dark green cloak blending him in with the shrubbery around them, so that Peter had to blink every so often to focus his eyes on him. When Pip had woken them up, grim faced as ever, he was wearing his leather armour, his thin sword at his side and a buckler hanging from his belt. Before they had left, he'd given Peter a sword, one of the four he had seen last night. Peter had attempted to say that he didn't know how to use one, but Pip had insisted on it, simply advising him to put the pointed end in the thing that was threatening him or Amys' life. That made him put it in his belt with great haste. If he needed to use it, he wasn't confident he'd be very effective, but he'd rather have it than not in case anyone did try to put Amys in any kind of danger.

They had walked for most of the morning until they saw the sun light pouring out in front of them. Peter turned to see that Amys was now fully sitting up and talking to the horse. They weaved through a few trees and then finally stepped out of the forest, and had the wonderful sensation of grass beneath their boots.

The forest grew at the beginnings of a slope, so as they exited, they had an excellent view of the valley of Carr, the sun shining upon it, warm and refreshing. The hill ran down into the valley undulating like an ocean in a storm. The valley itself was named after Mount Carr, a dark mountain to their left that grew into the sky, partially obscuring the view of the valley in its entirety. Running through the centre was a dirt path that ran its way to the town stead that was half cut off by the presence of the mountain.

They made their way through the hills, heading downwards by degrees, Pip navigating the route down before they stepped forward. Although Peter doubted Pip had ever been to this particular spot, Pip seemed very familiar with the terrain and the pattern of the landscape after only a few minutes of walking on it. They made quick progress down the hills, and as they did, the town stead of Little Carr came closer and closer into view.

It was built up around one central street that ran down the middle, connected directly to the dirt road that ran through it. The various buildings were not uniform in design, as they were each built at different times for various purposes. Peter couldn't remember much of what he had been told about the town stead's origins. There were a handful of new buildings added to it even from when he had moved there with his wife not ten years back, and he hoped for more in the future. They had all come from different places and different backgrounds, but Little Carr had become a home to each of them.

Behind the town stead, the road continued onwards into another forest, sparcer than the forest they had just left behind. The road continued into it and disappeared, curving round a bend. This road used to be a route that had a steady trickle of travellers going through it, and was the lifeblood that kept the people of Little Carr alive. The last ten days had seen a decline to the point of halting all travellers on those roads. News travelled fast apparently, and most merchants were willing to take the longer route rather than risk being robbed by bandits. Peter could not blame them for that choice. That is why they hoped Pip could do something about them. He deeply hoped.

They eventually got onto the road and Peter was glad to have home in sight. He gripped the sword again, the closer they came to it, his knuckles becoming white with every step. Amys evidently was looking forward to being in her own bed as she was bouncing up and down on Izzy's neck yet the horse steadfastly trotted onwards seeming to tolerate the young girl's excitement. The horse's master was also unaffected by the proximity of their destination. Pip simply continued forward at his usual pace, looking to either side of him taking in the location and the air. Peter attempted to follow whatever Pip was looking at, but his head turns seemed to be random. Was he just taking in the views, Peter wondered? There was probably something he was likely missing about the terrain that would be of some advantage to beating off the men in masks.

As they wandered into Little Carr, finally Peter allowed himself to feel relief that they had returned in one piece. Things were surely looking up. People in their store fronts stopped and stared at them as they walked through the town stead, pointing and for the first time in some time, smiling. People even tapped on windows, making the people inside come to their doors and join them in looking at the trio. Most eyes were drawn directly onto Pip, in particular, the weapons he was carrying, but he didn't seem to be fazed by the stares, or at least he had changed nothing about his demeanour. He wore same grim and set expression, his eyes scanning the buildings rather than the people, looking more at some buildings longer than others, but always moving on.

"Peter, where are we heading now?" inquired Pip turning to him fully, but always keeping his eyes on the buildings.

"We should head to Jackie's; she'll want to see that we're back in one piece," replied Peter, leading them forward into the around the centre of the main street.

There were two central buildings in the middle of Little Carr's single street, that being the church and a tavern. In most other villages, these two buildings would be almost rivals, but to Peter and most of the others who lived in the town stead, both were considered strong pillars of the community. That was primarily down to the two people who ran them.

As they walked up to the oblong tavern, a woman burst through the door and onto the wooden porch before them. Her brown hair was tied up in a loose bun, the various hairs that did not make it into the bun protruding in various directions. She wore a plain dress and an apron that was likely at one time white, but was now stained with various foodstuffs and liquids. Her shelves were rolled up and her face looked like thunder.

"Peter! I swear to high heaven if that little girl of yours has so much as a scratch!" she said marching down the stairs and directly towards them.

"Hey Jackie, I'm glad to see you!" exclaimed Peter.

He held out his arms for a hug, but instead he received a swift punch to the arm, as she walked past him and to Amys who was already shaking with glee to see the woman. Her face immediately softened when she saw the girl and she ran the rest of the way, plucking her off the horse and into her arms.

"I was worried sick about the two of you. You were gone for longer than a day and I feared the worst," she said holding Amys close to herself and spun her around.

After a few more moments of hugging, she let her down. The little girl scampered forwards toward the tavern, a familiar place for her.

"There were a few complications, but we found him," Peter said.

He gestured towards Pip who was already busy leading Izzy to a post near the tavern and taking off the various things attached to her saddle.

"I can see that. Will you help us?" she questioned looking Pip up and down, her lips pursed together as if she was going to say something but was forcing herself not to.

"I'll help," Pip responded, pulling the weapons tied in the blanket round his shoulder.

"He's a talker this one," she commented dryly to Peter then turned to Pip, "But by the looks of it, you know what you're doing with all of those weapons."

She walked up the two steps, her eyes trying to communicate something to Peter, but he didn't quite know if she was trying to make a joke or pointing out something very important that Peter should be aware of.

"Aye, I know what I'm doing with them," replied Pip following her up the steps, still looking around at the buildings.

"That's good to hear. We should talk then, but maybe without the audience," she said gesturing to the crowd of people that had gathered outside in causal groups of threes and fours, with their attention on the newcomer to town.

With that she headed inside, her hand over Amys' back, whispering something to her that made her giggle. Pip followed suit. Peter turned one more time to the crowd of faces that he knew well, smiled awkwardly, and then hurried to follow them inside, shutting the door behind him.

The interior of the Smiling Duck was very homely, with well-cleaned wooden tables, chairs and floors. There was a bar directly at the back of the Tavern, again well cleaned with mugs in wooden boxes around two barrels. There was a door round the side that led into a kitchen, double-hinged and had seen a lot of use. To the right was a staircase that led up to a second floor that ran round the establishment but could be fully viewed from the lowest floor. Each door was spread apart a reasonable amount to suggest a decent room within, but not so wide apart to give the impression of being too expensive to afford. The entire establishment gave the atmosphere of an orderly home.

Jacklin had already set Amys at one of the empty tables and had disappeared into the kitchen. Pip placed what had filled his arms and shoulder onto a table, and then added to it the various weaponry on his person, all the time scanning the room with his eyes making quick turns of the his head to see the full extent of it. Peter took a seat next to Amys, and sighed with relief, for the first time in the last two days, he could feel his muscles loosen.

Jacklin quickly returned, bearing in her arms a tray with three steaming bowls of soup upon it. She quickly noticed the items that now graced one of her tables and attempted to not make her face react, but Peter knew the frustration in her eyes, because it was usually being targeted at him. She placed the bowls on the table, laying them before Amys, Peter and an empty chair.

"It's not a lot, I'm afraid - we don't usually get customers at this time of day," she said apologetically glancing towards Pip.

She looked over to Pip hanging up his cloak on a rack provided at the door. She gave Peter another expression with her eyes, but again he didn't get what she was attempting to tell him, but decided it would better if he pretended he knew.

"This is perfect, thank you Jackie," he smiled.

Both she and Pip took their places at the table, and he finally turned his attention to Amys, who taken the soup being placed in front of her and had started eating. Peter couldn't blame her either; the smell was delightful and creamy with a nutty aftersmell that remained in the nostrils. He was ready to relax.

However, it didn't last for long. As soon as Peter had lifted a spoon to his mouth, a young man burst through the door, pale-faced and breathing heavily. He slammed the door as he came through it, turning his back to it, his eyes as wide as dish plates. Jackie was at his side, helping him up as quickly as she could, and even Pip got to his feet at the commotion.

"They're here. Three of them. White masks and with

weapons," trembled the young man breathing through his mouth as Jackie helped him to his feet.

Peter rushed to help her and laid him on a seat, which he collapsed on. While this was happening, Pip walked to the table where his packages lay, his expression unchanged.

As the young man lay there trembling there was a sound of slamming of doors. Peter stood up as these noises continued along the street, with various slamming echoing throughout their ears. He walked swiftly to one of the windows, and peaked through the blinds, his eyes locking onto the three dark figures that walked down the street. They walked directly in the middle of the path, their steps full of swagger and their weapons at their side. Peter could hear their coarse laughter as they walked through the street, becoming louder as they came ever closer to the centre of the town stead. They walked as if they owned every step they walked on.

"They're here all right, three of them," exclaimed Peter.

He turned back to the people in the tavern, his eyes having to search for a moment to see Pip at the table. As he approached Pip was picking up various weapons, testing their grips and then placing them down. Peter walked to his side, confused that Pip was not moving significantly faster.

"Are they armed?" asked Pip picking up a long dagger and sticking it behind his belt.

"Yes, I think one of them has an axe; the other two are armed but I couldn't see what they had, but they both hung from their belts," he replied his voice panic-stricken.

He watched Pip's very deliberate picking up and testing of the weapons.

"Probably maces," muttered Pip taking a broader sword, flipping it round in his hands to get his grip.

"What are you going to do?" asked Peter, but before Pip could answer, a voice cut through…

"We are here for one reason!" came the deep, haunting voice from outside, "We heard that one of you left a couple of nights back, and we thought we made ourselves very clear that you were forbidden to do that."

"I'm go to do what I've been asked to do," said Pip picking up in an axe with a single head.

"So, we've come to make sure you remember the rules!" the voice continued.

The silence of the town stead made the loud voice even more unnaturally intimidating. Pip walked to the door of the Tavern, his expression entirely unchanged.

"Hide Amys if you can - no child needs to see what happens next."

"What are you going to do?" repeated Peter dumbfounded the man's lack of intensity.

"Help."

And with that Pip opened the door, strode it into the empty street. Peter turned and saw that Jackie had heard his advice and was in the middle of taking Amys up the stairs. He then took a breath, gripped his sword and walked out to see Pip casually walking down the two steps in front of the tavern.

"Ah - finally someone is coming to talk to us," jeered the one at the front, holding his mace towards Pip, his dark face shining through the white mask.

Pip did not change his pace towards the three men and his expression remained set.

"Are those weapons? That's first for this backward town," he shouted and the other two men laughed to themselves.

Pip just continued, same pace, same expression.

"I hope you know how to use them, old man, because what comes next is going to hurt."

The man took his mace into both hands and the other

two began gearing up, but they were in no way ready for what happened next.

Striding forward, Pip threw the axe. It spun top over tail and lodged itself into the shoulder over the first man. The force impacted the man so hard, he staggered backwards, and fell, a scream bellowing from his lungs and red staining his black robes.

The other two men hardly had enough time to watch this happen before Pip was upon them, his empty hand now holding the long dagger. He made two strong thrusts at the masked man to his right, the first hitting his arm and the second being hit away by his axe, as he struggled to get away from the reach of the sword. Blood now poured out the wound and the man's teeth gritted, but Pip's face was still the same grim expression.

The third masked figure, who now had his own mace to hand, brought it above his head and down towards Pip's left side. He sidestepped it easily, thrusting forward with his dagger, making him jump back.

Pip then stepped immediately back to the one with the bleeding arm, thrusting and cutting in a series of blows that resulted in the man bleeding from his knee and face. A couple of the blows were deflected by the axe in both hands, but it seemed ineffective against the force that Pip was putting towards him with the blade.

The other masked man came in again, this time with two shorter blows, one to the side and then upwards. Pip avoided the first, but placed his boot on the second, resulting in the weapon flying from the man's hand. Pip then thrust the dagger into the man's chest, leaving it there, already ready turning to place his full attention on the man still standing.

This man with wide eyes saw his comrade fall and turned to see the other on the floor, an axe in his shoulder, whimpering with the pain. He decided he'd take his chances and flee, but as he started to sprint away, Pip was upon him, moving quickly for a man with greying hair. With a two-handed strike, he cut the man's side open, making him turn while he fell from the momentum. He then finished him with a swift blow to the neck, cutting off his death screams.

Pip then turned his attention to the man who was now crawling his way across the ground, his hand attempting to support the weight of the axe imbedded in his shoulder. When he saw Pip approaching him, sword bloodied and face grim, he screamed, his eyes shocked.

"Please no. We'll give you anything. Our leader is an influential man, he'll give you anything you want..."

His cries were cut off by a swift blow to the chest from Pip's blade, his begging and life cut short.

And just like that it was over. Peter only then noticed the fact that he hadn't even drawn his blade; he had been so mesmerised by what was taking place in front of him. It was nothing short of brutal, and it horrified him. He shook his head as he sheathed his weapon, knowing that he did not have the stomach for that kind of violence, especially if he was the one who was expected to inflict it. He looked back up to see Pip pulling the axe out of the corpse, and turned away again, the action and his stomach's reaction to it confirming what he had seen.

When he had the heart to look back up, Pip was cleaning his dagger on the robe of the dead man, , his eyes purely on the task at hand, his face grim and without change. When Peter looked up properly, he noticed that slowly doors and windows were opening, and people's faces were looking through them. Steadily people trickled out onto the street, whispering and pointing at the bodies of the men whom they feared so much, now motionless on the ground.

"We heard the screaming stop, what happened?"

demanded Jackie coming out onto the porch with Amys in her arms.

Her eyes answered their own question for themselves and her free hand lifted to her mouth to cover the fact that it hung open with shock.

More people came onto the street, even Father Michael came out of the church, holding his pendant and saying a prayer when he saw the bodies and blood covered dirt. They stood a few feet away, some with shock on their faces, others with fear. All looked at the figure of Pip now making his way towards the Tavern, all his weapons retrieved, and they all had hope deep in their eyes. Pip strode up the two steps, his expression totally unchanged from when he had left it only minutes before.

"What are you going to do next?" quizzed Peter meeting him as he got to the porch, waiting for any word of explanation or even a grand plan on how to defeat the masked men.

"Finish my soup," he replied.

With that he walked into the tavern without any waiting for any kind of response.

Peter's eyes followed him into the tavern, but quickly turned back to the people of Little Carr, still stood around the dead bodies. He exchanged glances with Jackie, who was keeping Amys' head close to her chest so that she did not have to see what was before them. He knew things would be different after this day. He wanted to be hopeful about the future of the town stead. As his eyes looked upon the corpses again, he wondered if there would be any reprisals.

# CHAPTER 8

## FARMERS IN ARMOUR

*S*inclair had been right about them not leaving right away. Tristan had woken up to an empty tent and the sun making its ascent into the sky. He quickly made his way out the tent, pulling on a shirt and stepped into the campsite. The bright light made him blink a few times to adjust. He looked around to see the ashes of the campfire where they'd left it the night before, with the men lying around it in various states of undress. As he walked out, he stretched, and some of the other men, looked up from their various positions of rest and greeted him with good mornings.

"Morning Tris, had a good sleep?" asked Jamie.

He walked over to greet him, a bowl in his hand and a cheerful smile on his face.

"All of me feels stiff," yawned Tristan, attempting to force himself to keep it in but that just made it worse.

"Well - get some of this in you and you'll feel better in no time," he assured.

He shoved the bowl into his hands, and Tristan murmured a thank you to him as he looked at its contents.

He supposed it was supposed to be porridge of some kind, but the smell was somehow under cooked and burned at the same time, something Tristan was unaware was possible, and the consistency rivalled that of building mortar. He put some into his mouth and immediately started coughing, as his body instantly rejected it.

"It will put hairs on your chest, that stuff," chuckled Frank from his position of lying on the grass, his shirt undone and beard untamed.

"Or you know, use it build a house," quipped Jeffery as Tristan once again attempted to take a mouthful and again his body rejected it.

The other men laughed and Tristan mentally noted to remember to take smaller spoonful.

"So, I'm guessing we're not marching today," observed Tristan.

He was attempting to get as little amount of the contents of the bowl onto his spoon while also trying to fill his empty stomach.

"Aye it looks like it. Herb and Harry went for a walk around the camp to see what they could find out. They're both used to trading with folks, being all good natured and the like, so they'll find out something by the time they come back," returned Jamie now sitting cross-legged, wittling a stick with his pocketknife, his tongue sticking out his mouth in concentration, but still with his good-natured face and playful eyes.

Tristan nodded to this reply, thoughtfully taking another scoop of porridge, but then thought better of it, putting most of it back into the bowl. He started to wonder what he'd do with however long they had to be at the camp. It had never really occurred to him that he could feel bored while being a soldier and a hero.

The answer to his predicament soon answered itself as

Joshua walked into the camp, his shirt drenched in sweat and cheeks red. He nodded in acknowledgment to Tristan as he went into the tent, and a few moment later returned with a fresh shirt on. His eyes were scanning the trees that were frequent within the valley and were until recently used as an orchard. Tristan followed them and they eventually reached one larger tree that stood only a short distance away.

"Tristan, I was thinking about the promise we made last night," he said his eyes still focused on the tree.

"Yeah, what about it?" answered Tristan.

He was more concerned with the way the other men looked towards the two of him when he mentioned the promise.

"I think one way I'll be able to keep it is by teaching you to defend yourself," he said his eyes still stuck on the tree.

"Won't we be given training of some kind when we reach the capital?" asked Tristan looking up to Joshua from his position on the floor.

"It's very unlikely - remember they're looking for men from villages not trained soldiers. They don't need us to be good at fighting, just good at dying," Joshua replied his Pickish accent, although lowered to conversational tones, seemed to carry its way further, and more than one man from other tents looked round at what he said.

Tristan was slightly taken aback by this answer, as he had been fully expecting to be a fully trained soldier by the time he left the capital. He also didn't like Joshua's references to death.

"May I borrow this?" asked Joshua pointing to the wood axe Jamie had lying next to him in the grass.

"You're welcome to it," offered Jamie in haste. He continued to carve, only quicker, his grip making his hand go white, but he still gave the same smile he gave everyone else, but Tristan thought that perhaps the man's eyes were a little dulled.

"Come on Tristan," ordered Joshua.

He picked up the axe and carried it by its head and began to make his way towards the tree his eyes had been fixed on for so long. Tristan looked to his porridge and looked back to Joshua's back, and decided which one would be more worth his time and effort. He hastily placed his bowl to the side and ran after the tall Pickish man. At least he knew with Joshua he wouldn't be sitting on his rear end all day.

They navigated their way through the tents, Joshua's eyes always scanning for the best possible route to the larger tree. Tristan gazed at the other men in the camp as they walked by them, and couldn't help but be disappointed. These were not fighting men in the armies of legends, they were farmers, shop keeper and tavern owners, or sometimes sons of men from these trades. Most looked in worse shape than the men from Tindale, their heads fully bald and red from the sweltering heat and their hairs on their chin greying. Some even found it hard enough work to get to energy to stand up, never mind pick up a weapon and go toe to toe with another man trying to take their life. Others still looked younger than he did, their hair curly and their faces scattered with freckles, their voices decidedly not dropped as they chased each other around the tents. Maybe Joshua was right, these were not soldiers, and it would be some time before they were.

Joshua's strides were long and swift, and many times Tristan had to do a short jog to catch up with him and keep his pace. But he'd always end up falling behind again and would have to catch up again. When they eventually got to the tree, he had to take a moment to breath as they both looked up at it. He had climbed larger, in fact, many trees larger than it, but compared to the other trees near it and across the valley, it was a giant. Its branches were low and gave off valuable shade, which many men took full advantage of, by sitting under it and speaking in low conversation, giving the two of them a nod of acknowledgement when they walked up to it.

"Do you think you could climb onto one of the lower branches and find two sticks roughly the length of my sword which won't snap after you hit them together?" asked Joshua.

He looked down to Tristan, after pointing to the lowest branch in sight. Tristan beamed with confidence, as a vast majority of his childhood had involved climbing up trees and finding sticks to turn into swords. He decided it was best to leave out the fact the Isabella, his usual opponent, would often beat him in these stick duels. Of course, he let her win. At least that's what he told himself.

"I'm sure I can; it's the getting the sticks off which will be the problem," said Tristan.

Tristan tried to act like he'd seen other men act when they conducted their business, but deep down he was excited that he got to do something that he hadn't done in some time.

"That's what the axe is for. Just get up the tree and I'll hand it to you, and you can use the blade to get sticks down," instructed Joshua.

He pulled up the axe into Tristan's eyeline, and Tristan even detected a small smile on his face as he did so. Maybe Joshua had enjoyed doing things like this when he was a child too, or maybe he was thinking about something else, it didn't really matter, what really mattered now was to get up the tree without looking like an idiot. Tristan brushed his hands together and ran forward, jumping up and wrapped his arms round the branch he was aiming for. He quickly pulled himself up and onto the branch, finding it a lot easier than he had when he was a younger boy - maybe all the helping his grandfather with the farm labour had really paid off. He looked down to see Joshua nodding approvingly and a few other men watching purely out of the fact that there was nothing else happening to interest them.

He pulled himself onto his feet, using the many other branches around him as balances, he walked forward to where the branches spilt off into smaller ones which had good stick potential. He lowered himself down, spreading his weight and legs across the branch. This was something that he'd missed about being a boy now he was considered a young man by many and here he was away from home rediscovering something he'd enjoyed.

"Can I have the axe now?" he asked lowering his hand for it.

Joshua apparently had been ready for the request as he almost immediately handed it up to him, the handle up.

"So, are you going to teach me to use a sword?" enquired Tristan.

He selected his first target and used the head of the axe to weaken it to the point of snapping.

"I doubt we'll get there. I want to teach you the movement of how to defend yourself when another man wants to take your life. That will do for now," answered Joshua.

He watched Tristan work intently, the hint of a smile gone now and his thoughts likely on things that Tristan didn't want to know about.

"I feel like one of the easier ways to stop a man from taking your life, is to take his before he can do you any harm," countered Tristan, snapping the branch off and throwing it to Joshua, who caught it out of instinct, snapping it out of the air.

"That could be considered true, but if you can avoid needing to take another man's life consider yourself blessed," he replied.

He looked at the stick that Tristan had thrown down to him, testing it in his hand.

"But isn't that the point of being a soldier though? Fighting and killing bad people?" questioned Tristan working on his next stick.

"Do you feel like a soldier Tristan? Or a boy from a village? I want to teach you enough to defend yourself when we see battle, but I wouldn't call many men here soldiers. It takes years of training to be a soldier, a real one, that is. Kings fight against so called usurpers throughout history, and their soldiers do the killing for them, and the people who die are people like us, taken from villages at the point of the sword and told we're fighting for the King. Do you even know who we're fighting against Tristan?" he asked.

Joshua's had been voice level throughout, but when Tristan looked down, his eyes looked like lightening, his face set in a stern expression that only yielded when he'd finished talking.

"I suppose. But there is a chance we could be heroes," remarked Tristan not really knowing how to respond to what he'd just said, letting the second stick fall.

"There's only two kinds of people, the dead and those who bury them," said Joshua.

He caught it and watched Tristan jump down from the branch.

"You know something Joshua?"

"What?"

"You can be really grim sometimes," said Tristan, a smile on his face.

For a moment Joshua didn't say anything, but his face turned into a smile and he let out a chuckle.

"You know what - Rosa says the same thing!" said Joshua actually smiling genuinely, his eyes shining while his head tilted up.

"She sounds like a wise woman," Tristan replied attempting nod in way a way he thought looked sage.

"She really is," smiled Joshua, handing one of the sticks to Tristan as they started back through the camp.

They walked their way through the camp, this time making as much light conversation as Joshua could make. They walked past the camp to drop off Jamie's axe, and then walked to the outskirts of the camp where there was a still a great deal of space left not taken up by tents. The grass was still green here, not yellow and trampled like it was in the centre of the camp, and it felt nice to be in the open for a while. Tristan even closed his eyes and let the wind blow into his face, pushing back his shaggy hair.

"All right then Tristan, let's get started while there is still light," he smiled.

He leaned on his stick, and Tristan turned to meet him.

"I know how to swing a stick; however, my guess is we aren't just going to be hitting each other with sticks," said Tristan spinning his stick in his hand.

"You guessed correctly. Although it may give me amusement to beat you even in a stick fight, but that isn't what we are going to be doing here. These sticks are going to be considerably lighter than any hand weapon you're given, but the way you defend yourself will be the same. The chances are when it comes to it, you will be able to deflect a deadly weapon," said Joshua taking his stick into his hand and balanced it again.

"Where to do we start?" Tristan pressed, bringing his spinning to an end, pointing his stick towards Joshua, closing an eye so he could look down it.

"Down here," he answered, moving his stick in front of him and gripping it with both hands, "You want to be able defend your head and torso at all times; you can live without your limbs, not so much without a head or beating heart."

81

"I don't know, I'm fairly certain at least a few of those men would be perfectly fine without a head," smiled Tristan moving his stick to copy the same position as Joshua.

"That's probably at least a little true," conceded Joshua smiling at the ground, and then with a speed that was beyond anything Tristan considered the man was able to do, thrust forward with his stick. Tristan had to step backwards, attempting to dodge the series of blows while also moving his stick to deflect them. By the end of the flurry Tristan had multiple hurting ribs, and a few scratches on his forearms and thighs.

"Well, that's a good place to start, I suppose," said Joshua.

He adjusted the stick in his hand, looked at Tristan with a little smile.

"Is there any place you didn't hit me?" asked Tristan breathing heavily his hands on his knees looking up at Joshua.

"I think you deflected a few, but you'll get better soon. All right again," said Joshua.

He moved forward with speed again and Tristan had to move quickly to the position he had been taught, immediately receiving a tap to one of his ribs. They continued like this until the sky turned orange, and Joshua decided it was time to stop for the day. Tristan felt numb all over, but by the end of the practice time, he felt like he was at least getting a little better. When they returned to the camp, the men had already started on dinner, and it wasn't long before he was sitting down with a bowl of hot stew in his hands, the numbness fading slowly the more he relaxed. This evening was like the others with laughter and joking, and Tristan found himself smiling throughout.

Herb and Harry had had quite the fruitful walk apparently, trading some of the Tindale supplies with the other recruits for things like soap and other more practical items.

They also found out that Joshua had been right in that the vast majority of the men and boys were from local villages, but they also claimed that there were also a large number from Camintar, a city on the coast not two days from the manor. These were apparently the people who had the most in trade, and by the smug grins Harry and Herb had when talking about it, he guessed they'd benefitted the most by the trades. He went to sleep that night happy but aching.

The next two days, he woke up stiff and bruised in places he didn't think he'd been hit. Nonetheless, he'd leave the tent every day to Joshua meeting him with a bowl of porridge and his stick. He considered it a good thing that he was doing it because at least he wasn't bored, and he was actually getting better, or at least a little better. Joshua had even decided that he could move onto other things with different foot works rather than pure reactional manoeuvres. Joshua even had to increase his attack patterns, which, of course, resulted in more bruises, but Tristan felt like these were significantly more earned. When the afternoons came, Jamie sat on the grass and watched them whilst carving at his wood with his knife. Joshua offered Jamie the same lessons as Tristan, but he'd always decline with a smile having seen the way Tristan looked by the time the lesson was over. Every day they saw the camps grow by a few tents, and new men trailing into the camp, usually escorted by three to four men on horses.

In the evening of the second day, the three of them walked into their camp and were handed their usual bowls of stew, and took their seats round the fire whilst Harry talked to people round the fire with the latest he'd heard from the soldiers themselves.

"And so, the order is that we're leaving in the morning, lads. One of the soldiers said the sergeants always get grumpy when people don't get packed quick enough and some start to get nasty, so I'd recommend getting ready early so we can avoid that," he finished.

All of this information could likely have been summed up in a few sentences, but he'd decided that it was worth spending the majority of their meal explaining it in the fullest of details. That night, their tent went to bed early and the next day woke with the sun, so they got a prime view of the soldiers going from tent to tent shaking men awake and ordering them to get packed and ready.

The march to the capital was uneventful in its monotony. Every day they'd wake up at the crack of dawn, the sergeants and soldiers would bark orders at the half-asleep farmers telling to get into rank and file, often intertwined with various insults. Then they marched until the sun was high the sky, have a two-hour break, and then continue to match until the sun was nearly setting. Then in the evening Tristan spent his time learning a little from Joshua and sitting in front of the campfire remembering the not so long days ago where he didn't have to go anywhere in a hurry or walk very far. But he reminded himself that one day this would be worth it, and he also promised himself not to focus on this part when he told it back to a captive audience.

This routine continued for ten days, and every man by the end of it had blisters a-plenty. There were however, a few silver linings to the particularly dark grey cloud which broke up the constant feeling of having to force one foot in front of another. For one thing, Joshua said Tristan was getting better at defending himself, although Tristan thought that he was going a little easier on him since the marching started, but he was happy to hear it. Another thing was sometimes the army would make camp outside or within walking distance of a village or city, and Herb and Harry would go in the trade with them, then come back into the camp and trade with the men there. It meant that their tent always had a supply of good things, and they were treated with favour by the other men and soldiers alike.

However, the thing that made it worth every single step they'd travelled was the view of the capital. The land in the last two days leading up to it was flat, so on the horizon there began to appear a white dot. As they kept on marching towards it, the dot became larger but still mostly undefined to Tristan no matter how much he squinted. Slowly as they came closer, the white walls of Tylander became completely visible. They grabbed the eyes of man; even Joshua looked impressed by the sheer magnitude and scale of the walls. Legend said they were forged by the breath of Metallic Dragons before they flew to the heavens, and Tristan could well believe it. Even while they were still miles away, they stood tall to his vision, with watch towers placed throughout, standing even taller that the wall itself, each one's top pointed like a mountain.

That view certainly made the men step faster; it became a target to their marching. They even started singing marching songs in the last half day that it took them to get to Tylander, as most of the men's spirits were raised enough to sing songs worth singing. When they'd marched until about midday, they came over a small hillock in the road and before them was Tylander in full scale of intimidating magnificence. The walls loomed even larger from that close perspective, and as the men walked, the larger they became. The walls them-selves were round leading from the sea either side with a colossal gate set in the middle. Around the city was a sea of tents, all made from the same off-white material. Tristan could not believe his eyes when he saw the vastness of the army. He didn't quite know who they were fighting against, but he was confident that what he was seeing in that moment was the largest army in the world.

They were led down into the camp, and were instructed

to make camp with five tents per campfire to conserve space. Tristan was in awe of the huge scape of blue that he could see if he stood on top of a raised part of the ground. He'd never seen anything like it before, and every time he'd finished with a job, he'd go back to looking at it. The sunlight danced on clear blue water like countless jewels and it took his breath away. It was worth all the marching.

The campfire that night was crammed with men that Tristan didn't recognise, so he made sure to sit in between Joshua and Jamie during the time they were preparing and eating their evening meal. Tristan tried to look over as much as he could to the ocean, but as the sun went down, the water became an immense, dark expanse. After a little while of sitting at the fire, conversation struck up between the men, and soon the laughter and storytelling began, with Harry in the middle of it all, talking and laughing with men he'd only met that day like they had been friends their entire life. Some of the stories that the men told were simply repeats of others he'd heard, but there were one or two that made him sit up and listen.

He went to sleep that night with the sounds of the ocean in his ears like a soft lullaby, holding his blanket close to himself, as the night seemed a little colder than usual on the outskirts of Tylander. He was now truly far from Tindale, and he was excited for what the next day held.

# CHAPTER 9

## A MESSAGE

*J*acklin had never seen the Smiling Duck as full as it was that evening. The entire town stead had decided to celebrate the events of the day, and so as the sun had gone down, the people - both adults and children alike - trickled into the tavern. She had a feeling that something like that would happen, and so brought in the usual help that she hired at the weekends and also the young man named Jacob who had nearly passed out on the floor earlier. The four of them licked place into shape with the help of Peter and Pip, although Jacklin grumbled that they hadn't helped nearly as much as they could have, only putting out the extra chairs in from the store house and rolling in an extra cask of ale. Yet no matter how much she prepared, Jacklin could not have visualised just how many people made up Little Carr, and how stress-inducing they could be when they were all together.

Jacklin stood in the door of the kitchen, her eyes scanning the floor that she had so meticulously cleaned that morning, her eyes cringed at all the food and liquid that had been dropped or spilt there. She looked at all the faces, now filled with hope and even happiness. Her face though was creased with anxiety with the amount food that they could possibly serve and whether they'd have enough ale. Thankfully everyone accommodated Father Michael, who went from table to table talking to people in his loving way, and placing half-filled mugs onto trays and also talking to the men about the value of teaching their children good habits through example, which made them drink a little slower.

She let her eyes wander throughout the room and found their rest on Amys who was yawning while sitting on her father's lap, and she felt herself smile. Peter doted on that girl, and Jacklin couldn't blame him in any way; she was a good-natured child and had a lot of her mother in her even at her young age. Jackie had always had a close relationship with Sarah, and so she felt the responsibility to be a calming influence on both Amys and Peter, but apparently she wasn't as effective as she thought because he'd still taken her with him on his foolish search for someone they weren't certain existed. Yet Pip did exist, but it was still a foolish thing to do, she thought.

"Miss Jacklin?" she heard a voice saying from behind her.

She turned from her looking to seeing one of the young woman named Hannah who worked for her on the weekends.

"What's the problem Hannah? If it's someone complaining about the portion sizes again, I will be happy to explain to them what it's like to cook for this many people," she quizzed her hands returning to her hips and already preparing the speech she might need to make to whomever stirred her frustration.

"Well, that's the thing Ma'am - there's nothing left to do," said Hannah, glancing back to the other two who were still in the kitchen, egging her on.

"Nothing?" she repeated arching one of her eyebrows.

The concept of nothing left to do of one that was entirely foreign to her; there was always something left to do.

"Well, apart from the collecting and washing of dishes, but we've got that covered for you," she said earnestly.

Jacklin could see beyond her watching the other two nodding in complete agreement. She then looked back in the room. Things had certainly de-intensified; people sitting where they could, their bellies full and they were also starting to nurse their drinks rather than take swigs from them. She, of course, also felt tired, but she always felt tired so that wasn't anything new. The offer was still a tempting one.

"I will go out for some fresh air, and then I will be straight back,' she said reluctantly and then fiercely, "You'd better have those dishes spotless by the time I come back!"

The three helpers all responded in celebration, but when she raised her eyebrow to this, they all set about looking busy.

Jacklin made her way to the door, weaving in and out of people to get there. They all knew her, so as she walked past people they'd attempt to make friendly conversation. However, her years of needing to finish jobs and serve drinks had meant she'd mastered the friendly one sentence answer, smiling ever so politely. But her answers and body move-ments away from people often allowed her avoid conversa-tions without being considered to be rude. She knew rudeness led to people being offended, and offence was bad for business.

After a few smiles and pushes, she managed to slip out the door and close it carefully behind her. Once she was out, she took a deep breath of the cool air, letting it fill her lungs up, and then when she breathed out, all her stresses seemed to go with it. She wandered over to the railing of her porch taking off her apron and she felt like her body could relax for a moment. Her apron was on her body so much of the day, it had learned that taking it off meant it then didn't have to function at full capacity, which was a lovely feeling. She looked out onto the street of Little Carr, most of it shrouded in darkness, but from the lanterns that hung off the tavern, she could make out some of it. She laughed a little to herself that this time one day ago she would have been terrified to step one foot out the door at night, but a day can change a lot of things, as the people now filling her Tavern could testify to.

She rested her elbows on the railing, and let her neck loosen, resting her head on her hands. Without even thinking, her eyes looked to her left, and she almost screamed when she saw a shadowy figure sitting on the two steps leading up to her porch. Jacklin was fully prepared to scream, but she recognised the greying face and worn boots of Pip and settled herself. He hadn't seemed to notice her coming outside as he was fully occupied carving into a block of wood while sitting across the stairs.

"It's a very lovely evening Pip, wouldn't you agree?" observed Jacklin.

She didn't really know what to say to the man, but also knew that she couldn't not say anything to the man who had taken the first steps towards liberating the town stead that afternoon.

"Yes, very nice," he responded.

He did not even look up from his work, but seemed not to be surprised that she was there, so she guessed that he had been aware of her presence, but just hadn't spoken.

"They all think you're a hero; I don't think they're all crowding into my Tavern for my cooking. They're here for you," she said, looking out into street, remembering the looks on people's faces and even the feeling she had in her own heart.

"I don't think I'm a hero," he said shortly.

He stopping carving for a moment to look into space with the same grim expression, but then continued on with his carving.

"Well, I guess you don't get a huge choice in the matter. Why did you come if not to become a saviour of the people?" she asked, a hint of frustration in her voice.

No one did the kind of thing he did for free. Such men would bask in the good graces of the people and then he'd take their wealth in the same way the masked men did. Just when he took it, people would do it smiling rather than at sword point. That's what she was thinking.

"I came to help."

"Do people like you do what you're doing for free? Help suggests that there's some charity in it," she said.

She gazed at the man almost surprised at herself for saying the things she was letting come out of her mouth. But these were all the things that had been bouncing around her mind since that afternoon, and she was too tired to put on a real filter for the man.

"You seem like a very honest woman Jacklin, and so I'll be honest with you. I'm not doing this for charity, I'm doing it for a friend."

He looked at her with his dark eyes which looked straight through her. Jacklin was convinced this was the longest sentence, the grim man had ever said, and so she was keen to keep it going.

"So, you consider Peter a friend?"

"No. No. I'm helping because of an old friend. Although Peter seems like he's very agreeable man, I doubt I'd be here if he was the only factor in me coming here," he confided looking to the sky for a little, but then quickly went back to his carving.

"So, do you know who these masked men are? Did they

hurt your friend? Is that why you're here, to get revenge?" she quizzed bolting straight upright, her head filled with more questions than those.

"I've come across them before, just not in the way they're doing things here," he said.

He looked over the wood block he had been putting notches into and then blew onto it.

"Aren't they simply just bandits who happen to want to take us for all we're worth? Just doing it in white masks and a leader who can turn the sky the colour of midnight?" she asked, looking out into the street half expecting a white masked man to come out of the shadows towards her.

"They are certainly acting like it," he responded.

He placed the piece of wood in his belt and pushed the knife blade into the handle.

"Are they more than that?" she asked afraid of the answer that came next.

"They themselves are likely just to be brigands and ruffians, especially by the way they fight. But who is leading them and who they are claiming to be by wearing those masks means they are a lot more than that," he replied.

He twisted himself round so he was simply sitting forward on the steps his face in the shadows of the night and Jackie could no longer see his expression. She supposed it would be as grim and set as ever.

"What are they claiming to be? What do those masks mean?" she asked walking over to the stairs to get closer to read the look on the man's face, but all she really got was a better view of his back.

"I've lived by the sword most of my life, and the chances are I'll die by it, whether it's tomorrow or the next day or the day after. I've seen things that most men have nightmares about. I'm not a good man by any means. But what those masks mean and what they're connected to is evil. Pure and simple."

Pip's voce was level, but there was something in them that made Jacklin shiver and clutch her apron close. She could've sworn the air around her got colder around her, but Pip hadn't changed his stance; his eyes simply stared into the darkness.

"Do you think you'll be able to do something about them?" asked Jacklin.

The hope that she didn't know she had slowly slipping away from her the more her mind dwelt on the thought of Pip considering something evil. Especially after seeing the aftermath of that afternoon.

"I will do what I can to help," said Pip standing to his feet and stretching, eyes still focused on the darkness.

"I am assuming that means more people will die," she said.

She tilted her head to the side, studying him closely. Pip may be a dangerous man, but he also carried something else about him that she couldn't put her finger on.

"That's usually the way it goes," he observed turning to lock her eyes, his brown eyes deep set and she put her finger on it.

Pain. He carried pain in his eyes at all times.

"I think all of that can wait until the morning, don't you Pip?" she pointed out seeing the man standing before her, scarred and grim, in a totally different light.

He had a weight on his shoulders that would break a normal man. Maybe Pip wasn't a normal man.

"Well, there isn't a lot we can do about it now is there. You should probably get back in there - I heard at least two plates breaking," he said in casual tones, his face still set in place with the usual grim look.

She wanted to talk more to try and help the man in some way, but he didn't look like someone who would be helped easily. That and the ears of the person who broke the plates weren't going to box themselves...

She left Pip outside as she tied her apron onto herself, her lack of hope restored but also something more than that. The man outside on her porch was more than what he seemed to display and she was determined to understand who he was, deep down.

The night went on and she was sure that people would have lingered all night in the Tavern if she hadn't asked Father Michael to politely ask people to leave. They left with smiles on their faces and hope in their eyes, and she truly didn't have it in her to tell them to think otherwise. Everyone had left before she saw the full destruction in their wake. Then that's when the real work began, tidying up the mess. Thankfully she wasn't alone as she had her three workers and Peter and Father Michael to help tidy things away. Pip even came in and moved some chairs, the same expression on his face. By the time everything was finished, all were exhausted and ready to sleep. Her last thoughts before dropping off to sleep were of all things that she had to the next day before she could even think about opening her doors.... and Pip. The words he had said bounced around her head, but what really stuck her was the deep pain in his eyes. How could anyone bear that without breaking?

Jacklin's sleep was filled images of masked men and all the terrible possibilities of who they were really, which meant it was all the more disturbing when she woke up to the sounds of explosions. They continued to echo in her mind as she shook herself awake. She leapt out of bed and pulled on her dressing gown, rushing down the wooden stairs. Peter emerged from his and Amys' room that they had been staying in that night, concern written all over his face. Pip was apparently already awake and looking out of the window, fully armoured, the usual expression on his face. Did the man ever sleep?

"What happened? I heard the sounds of something explosions and I came," she said, trying to look out of the blinds while tying her dressing gown properly.

"They've arrived," he commented.

He flung open wide the door and stepped out letting the light of the early morning inside and revealing the view of eight figures all dressed in black with snow white masks covering their faces, turning to face the tavern.

Even in the daylight, their presence was intimidating, whether it was because of their shadow-like dress or their various weapons, it was hard to tell. All except their leader, whose mask covered the entirety of his face. At that moment, his finger was pointing deliberately at the sky.

Pip walked onto the porch staring the eight men down like they were simply eight ordinary people, rather than masked bandits who had their numerous weapons drawn with murderous smiles. Jackie was really starting to believe the part he had said about nightmares.

"Well, if it isn't our favourite town hero, come to save this backwards dump," mocked the leader.

He brought his finger from its position in the sky, and opened his arms to gesture the whole town stead. By this time every one of them was awake, only courageous enough to peek through their blinds at what was happening in the centre of the street.

"I'll have you know that you're not wanted here," announced the leader, "Not wanted at all."

"Now this is a warning you leave this town by sunup tomorrow or we kill you," he continued, "Right in the middle of the street. We're going to make yesterday look like a picnic."

"And right when we're finished, we'll dump you in front

of the church, so people will know what happens when you try to be a hero!" he, and his men jeered throughout his little speech, but Pip keep his eyes locked on them, unflinching, unmoving.

"Well, then are you going to say something? Or has all your little courage gone from yesterday?" he screamed at Pip and his men continued to throw threats in the general direction of him.

Yet Pip remained the same, staring them down, his expression grim and his eyes set.

"Maybe a sign will loosen your tongue," he threatened.

The leader pointed his finger into the sky and shouted some words that Jackie did not recognise. Then from his finger, a streak of red flew into the sky. Jackie's eyes followed it up and then to her utter shock, it exploded into a colossal ball of fire. It was high enough above the buildings not to damage them, but she could still feel the wave of heat that came from it. Yet Pip stood still, barely even moving his neck to view the explosion of fiery colours.

"You are a fool like everyone else in this town. Leave by tomorrow or we will kill you in the most painful way we can think of. And believe me, it will be a pleasure to do so," he vowed repeating his threat looking to Pip and seemed disappointed by his lack of movement.

The leader then told his men to get in close and said some other words that Jacklin couldn't hear. After this, their cloaks seemed to grow and grow until shadows took up the entire street, totally consuming them, then suddenly the sunlight appeared again as if it had never been covered. Then where there once stood the black robed men, there was simply street.

Jacklin let out the breath, she had been holding in and stepped out onto the porch, Peter quick on her heels. The people of the town slowly opened their doors, again stepping out, but they stayed nearer to their houses than the day before. Pip stood in the same position that he had been throughout, staring at where they had disappeared into shadow, yet now he had a smile on his face, something that was a first for Jacklin to see. At least she thought it was a smile; he was obviously out of practice with smiling.

"Why the change in look? I'd say you looked almost happy," she exclaimed.

Peter looked shocked that she talked to him in this way, but she imagined he would be as curious as she was to that reaction to the display of power.

"They have no idea what they're doing," he said still looking to where they'd turned into shadow.

"They blew up a fireball to prove a point and they also have those weapons which aren't a laughing matter," pointed out Peter trying to follow Pip's eyeline into the street but wasn't seeing anything new.

"If they knew what they were doing, they would have killed me where I stood; they outnumbered me eight to one, but they didn't. The leader also doesn't know why he's here," Pip said matter-of-factly them turning from where he was looking to the two people in front of him, his face returning to his usual expression.

"Is that a good thing?" asked Peter as Pip walked past him and into the tavern, his and Jacklin's eye exchanging looks of confusion.

"It's interesting," murmured Pip drawing his long dagger holding it into his gloved finger, testing the sharpness of the weapon.

"It's interesting? Pip you're going to have to give us a lot more than that, I'm afraid. The people out there in the town - they need to know that they're going to be safe tomorrow. Because you gave them a glimmer of hope, and now that's fading away very quickly. I have a feeling that tomorrow if nothing changes, you aren't the only one who's going to die. What are you going to do?" Jackie demanded, her voice changing swiftly from frustrated to fearful. How any person could smile in the face of such things wasn't right; it simply wasn't.

"I'm going to help."

"How?" she demanded again, her arms folded across herself and she could feel her cheeks burning.

"I'm going to kill every last one of them," he replied, no anger, no rage, just pain in his eyes.

Pip then put the dagger behind his back and walked back up the stairs and went to his room. Jackie's eyes followed him and watched as the door closed. The truly odd thing was that even after seeing what she had just witnessed, the fire and the shadow, she actually believed that he was going to do just that. It was a strange feeling, and it didn't make her feel particularly good, but she know that Pip would kill every last one of them. Maybe that's what hope feels like.

# CHAPTER 10

## TO WAR

Tristan quickly dodged Joshua's stick, leaning back, and then lifted his stick up to hit away the next blow which came quickly jabbing his own stick forward in a thrust. This attack was, of course, very quickly hit to one side, but Tristan didn't mind that much because at least he got the attack off. The two continued in their sparring, Tristan on the defensive most of the time but every so often he got some parries in, although none of them landed.

The two of them had continued their daily habit of moving a little way from the camp to practice with their sticks, this time with the added benefit of the beautiful view of the city and the ocean. It had been ten days since they arrived in front of Tylander and the men had already fallen into a routine of sorts: waking and sleeping at regular hours and attempting to stay cool by any means at their disposal.

The two who had adapted the quickest were, of course, Harry and Herb as early on the morning of the first day being there, they had any metal or tool taken from them by grim faced soldiers, apparently to aid in the making of weapons for all the men. This meant that many people's items that had some value to them were taken, and that's when Harry and Herb did their best work, making some kind of deal with the soldiers to get the smaller trinkets back trading them for favours and other valuables with the rest of men. They had then managed to find a way into the city, even though that was forbidden, and they laid their hands on some very luxurious items.

"You're certainly improving," concluded Joshua.

They finished their exercise, both sweating, but even Joshua smiled as they headed to where Jamie was sitting as a one-man audience.

"Well, maybe you're just getting worse," Tristan smiled.

Deep down, he was glad to hear he was improving. He was certainly returning to the camp with less bruises.

"It looked very good from here, however, that's coming from someone who doesn't know a lot about hitting people with sticks," observed Jamie sitting up properly as they approached, his usual friendly demeanour about him as he threw a canteen to Tristan, who caught it, gulped the luke-warm water and let it run down him to cool him.

"Well, your father certainly knew how to hit people with sticks," added Tristan throwing the canteen to Joshua, who was equally grateful for the cooling liquid.

"Aye that's true. But that was only if you got caught," laughed Jamie.

He leaned back onto the grass and looked out onto the ocean. Tristan joined him on looking out on the water. The sun was making its descent down the sky, but there was still plenty of light left. That light bounced in and out of the waves which crashed forwards as they spashed onto the shore. It was mesmerising and then they lay in silence for a moment just watching.

"This reminds me of the ocean in Malancore. When the sun hits off it, the entire thing looks like one giant shimmering blue sapphire," reminisced Joshua, his eyes still looking steadily at the vast ocean.

This was the first time that Joshua had said anything like that since the first night at the campfire, and Jamie and Tristan looked round at Joshua hoping there would be more.

"Do you have any other stories from your days in Malancore?" probed Tristan leaning to try and get a view of his eyes.

"None that you would be interested in," Joshua looked forward for a moment, and then turned to smile at the two other men.

"I don't know, I feel like there's a few stories in there somewhere. Like how a member of the elite guard of Malancore ended up living in a town like Tindale. And how someone like you ended up with such a beautiful a wife," said Jamie leaning back again, like what he was saying was the most casual thing in the world to ask a man about his life story.

"Well, they are both somewhat related to each other," said Joshua and stroked his chin with one hand his eyes back to the ocean.

"Wait - was she the reason you had to leave?" exclaimed Tristan leaning forward interestedly.

His mind was racing with the crazy possibilities was what that could mean. The wildest that came to his head was that she was some kind of princess in the Malancore harem, and they fled in the night to escape the King.

"In a way she was, but again, it's not as glamorous as you might think," said Joshua again smiling to himself and looking forward.

"Try us," grinned Jamie leaning fully back his head on the grass and the sun shone onto his face.

"Elite guards are strictly speaking not meant to get married. That's why they bring people from other kingdoms to serve in the palaces. Ladies-in-waiting are also not meant to get married while in they are in service, due to children distracting from their work. Both things that two people in love don't find appealing," Joshua replied matter-of-factly

"So, Rosa was a hand maid, you two fell in love, got married and ran away. Then in some way you ended up in the empty farmhouse near Tindale," said Tristan putting together the elements of what he said.

"Something like that,' said Joshua pushing himself up onto his feet and looking down at the other two. "Come on - we should get back to the camp, unless you two prefer sunbathing?"

Tristan immediately sprang to his feet, and then he and Joshua dragged Jamie to his feet.

The three then walked together talking about this and that as they stepped through the grass. They came over a small hill and could see a view of the whole camp with the intimidating city walls, glaringly white in the sunlight. They stood still for a moment to take it all in. Then the huge gates to the city began to open. The three men stayed where they stood, their eyes gazing at something that they could barely believe was real. Something that looked like a dragon leapt on top of the gate, its rider in red and gold, his lance raised high. Then what came through the gate took their beath away. Giant mounts that strode forward, with rows of scales covering them, colours of fire, their teeth like razors and eyes like demons. Their riders were wearing the same red and gold armour, elegantly crafted, their long dark hair flowing behind them. They walked out in pairs, their strides echoing.

"Are those elephants?" asked Tristan his eyes glued to the creatures as they kept on walking forward, and behind them were ranks of foot soldiers in the same armour, their spears reaching high in the sky and their elegant swords at their sides.

"They are drakes, ridden by Fire Elves," explained Joshua bitterness hanging off his voice with every word.

"Not a fan of Fire Elves?" enquired Jamie his eyes very much glued on the vast army pouring out of the gate, "I heard the King is half one."

"My grandfather fought against them in the wars in the north under King Alexander's father. He lost a leg to their fire magic as they turned the floor to lava. He would tell me stories of their horrific beasts and terrible warriors who were worth three men. Then our hero King Alexander married one of them. Now our King is a half-elf, and our army is made up of those who my grandfather gave his blood for," lamented Joshua his eyes watching the ranks on ranks of elves walking out of the gates. They were then followed by the knights of Tylander and the men dressed in the armour and crests of Alexander.

"Maybe it's better? At least they're on our side?" asked Tristan not sure about what he was saying as he said it, his eyes still glued to the massive army, "Who could stand against such a force?"

"They aren't on our side. The men above us aren't on our side. They start wars for our own good apparently, for the defence of the kingdom that we have no ownership of, then a couple of years later become allies with the very people they fought against. The men above us don't die or suffer or lose anything. We are the wolves of war, and they drive us ahead of them to die," said Joshua his face as dark as his tone, his eyes burning red like the armour of the elves who were marching out of view now.

"I think it would be best if we head back into camp now. If they're leaving, we can't be far behind them," said Jamie forcing a smile, but his eyes didn't match it and they seemed equally grim as Joshua's face.

The other two men started walking down towards where their tents were pitched, and Tristan looked back at the army still filing out of the city, not really understanding the words that Joshua spoke, not sure he wanted to understand.

The three men walked down into their camp to the sound of a great commotion. Men in armour were organising the men from the camp into lines, and they realised they had come back just in time as the first line of men were being sent off towards the armoury. They quickly joined the line of the men they recognised as their friends.

Tristan could hear himself beathing and his heart racing inside his chest. This was it - he was going to war.

When it was the turn of his line to start moving, they made their way towards the capital, where the armoury was located, a fairly straight path through the tents. As they walked through the camp, the faces of the men around them looked like they were mourning. They already wore the roughly made armour that was being handed out and carried the crudely made weapons loosely in their hands. When they got into the tent, each man was given some armour. Tristan was handed a chainmail shirt and a helmet that looked many sizes too large for him by a man who looked like he would rather be doing anything else but that task. He then walked forward and was handed a shield that he could barely carry and an axe that nearly fell out of his hand the moment he held it. He was then shunted out the other end of the tent wondering what to do next. Joshua found him, and led him back to the campsite, carrying his chain shirt and shield, but in his hand was a spear, not as long at those carried by the elves but long enough that it reflected the sun every time Tristan tried to look up at it.

They arrived back at their tents with all the other men,

each carrying armour of some description, a weapon for both the hands or a single-handed weapon and a shield. They all looked somber as at a funeral, and they stood around as if waiting for instruction. Joshua disappeared into the tent and a moment later came back out with his sword tied to his side and a helmet from Malancore on his head. He looked quite the warrior. He then proceeded to instruct the men on the best way to wear the armour and how to use their weapons. They all listened attentively, without even muttering a word; even Harry stayed quiet. Last of all, he came to Tristan and even gave him a little smile.

"Now this is a bit different than what we've been practicing with, but the principle is the same. Keep your shield up, protect your body. The axe is a lot more of a hacking weapon, so make sure you remember that when it comes to it," he said showing Tristan how to hold the weapon, balancing it in one hand.

"Do you remember our promise, Joshua?" reminded Tristan.

He was trying not to shake with what he called excitement, but maybe it was fear.

"I remember it well. You'll get me back to see Rosa and I'll get you back in one piece," promised Joshua with a deep seriousness, and his mouth opened again as if he was going to say something, but someone else walked into the camp, with an escort of soldiers around him.

"All right men - I need these tents cleared away as quick as possible. We'll probably be the last to leave but we're leaving," said the man, with a fine combed moustache that twirled up both sides of his face.

He wore a blue coat with fine leather armour beneath and a beautiful sword at his side, with a thin blade and a guard fashioned with intricate craftsmanship. He had a flask in his hand that he was taking a swig of as they came in and then as

105

he turned to leave, took another swig, muttering something about, even if it's midnight, we'll still be leaving.

Joshua looked back to the men and they all silently got to work, taking down the camp. Already as Tristan went into their tent, the far reaches of the camp was already being taken down and the men were forming into ranks by soldiers on horses. Tristan pulled his rucksack up and took out the long dagger he'd been keeping there for some time, held it in his hand and then pushed it into the back of his belt. Then he pulled everything into it and walked out. Even more of the camp was being taken down and men quickly were put into ranks, their faces grim as they marched forward. Tristan tried to help where he could, but he was distracted by all the thoughts turning over and over in his head. He was going to be in a battle, and he was going to be a real soldier, and he had no idea if that excited him or terrified him.

They were one of the last groups to be finished, but the sun still had light to it, and they were shuffled into a larger group of men. Then the man with the moustache rode up to them on a white horse, looked over them once and then turned to the road, taking a large swig from his flask. Then with that, they were marching forward, onto the wide road and away from the capital.

This leg of marching was easily the hardest for Tristan and for the other men around him. It wasn't the path - it remained very flat with only a few inclines - it was the weight of their armour and weapons constantly pushing down on them, reminding them of their presence at all times. There was no talk from among the men, as they were all gritting their teeth to deal with the weight. Tristan tried to listen out for the sounds of talk from anywhere, but neither the group before them nor behind them made any sounds except marching.

When the sun was beginning to truly sink, they reached a

fork in the road. Tristan could see the rest of the army turning up and to the left, but the unit before them turned to the right and turned East. Tristan was too exhausted to voice any of his questions out loud when they turned to the left with them, but he looked around him and all the other men all wore his confusion in their eyes and yet they kept on marching, hoping they would stop soon. Yet it was almost another full hour of marching before they did stop for camp at the side of the road near a small patch of trees.

The men set up camp quietly, with the odd conversation here and there, but most didn't have the energy for it. As some put up the tents, others were sent to get firewood from the patch of trees, and soon fires started dotting up around the camp. Harry and Herb produced some of the extra food they'd kept from their trades and added it to the rations they were given, to create what Tristan truly believed to be the best tasting food he could ever remember tasting. It didn't have anything particularly special in it, but it was hot and filling and that's all it needed to be for Tristan to regard it as perfect. The men ate it gratefully staring into the firelight.

"Do you mind if I join you?" asked the man with the thin twirling moustache, walking into the firelight.

None of the men had any energy to object as the man sat down amongst them, taking out his flask. He offered to the other men, who didn't make enough movement to accept it. He then shrugged and then took a swig.

"I guess you might be all wondering what we're doing here, separating from the army and all. Also, the names Ulysses, in case any of you were wondering," he continued, as if he wasn't wearing a fine coat and a beautiful sword, and was just like the men sitting in front of him were old friends.

"Rumour said that the war was to be nearer the north border to Tagon," countered Harry, looking into his bowl thoughtfully, very much a new look for him.

"Correct. That's likely going to be where the initial clashes will take place, however, there has been rumour of some Tagon and Divinera outriders crossing the border. Not enough to be any kind of threat to the capital, but enough to disrupt supply lines with the capital, and so we've been sent to scare them back into going back over the border," informed Ulysses.

"Tagon raiders this far south? How is that possible? I always thought those two Kingdoms were not on friendly terms," said Joshua talking to Ulysses as if he were his peer.

"Well, ordinarily you'd be correct, but since one of the first things Alexander did as King was march in and behead the Lord Supremis, his son and the High Priest, accusing them of being traitors, Divinera started having a less than friendly view of the current monarchy, and his son only made things worse with his heavy taxes of imports. It also helps that the would-be King is claiming to be born of the daughter of the aforementioned Lord Supremis and Alexander himself. That makes them two allies because they both happen to have the same enemy," Ulysses explained casually as if it was something they all should know.

"How come you're so knowledgeable about this all? You talk as if it's common knowledge," pressed Frank.

"Ah yes, sorry, my apologies. Sometimes I forget. To think I came here to get away from that all that," he apologised taking a long swig from the flask and looking into the fire for a moment.

"No need to apologise. It's nice to know who we're actually fighting," said Harry leaning back onto his rucksack and gazing into the night's sky.

"It doesn't change anything though, does it? We're fighting for someone who got us here at sword point in a conflict that doesn't truly affect us. We are the wolves of war, driven before their horses, and it's us who will make up the dead not them," said Joshua bitterly, looking into the fire alongside Uylsses, and the rest of the men's eyes darting between the two men.

"He's not wrong. Men like King Al-cander use men like my father to be the general for armies made of men that will in no means benefit from the conflict they're involved in. Don't over think it though, do something more productive with your time like drinking," advised Ulysses.

He drained the last drops from his flask. He shook it a few times over his mouth but only a few drops got into his mouth, which he seemed most disappointed about.

"Well - I should be heading anyway; the earth is already shaking. Glad to meet you all, especially you young man. Cheerio."

He excused himself struggling to get into his feet, but he put up his hand in refusal of any help when the men around him attempted to balance him. The way he'd referenced Joshua made Tristan remember how young he was, but the bags under his eyes and the weight in his words always made him appear to be older. Ulysses stumbled into the night, tripping a few times as he made his way through the tent.

"So that's the man leading us? Maybe his suggestion for a pastime wasn't so bad," mumbled Stephan under his breath.

But he received a quick nudge in the ribs from Jamie. When he began to object, he noticed Jamie's eyes towards to Tristan and silenced himself.

"It's not really worth focusing on all the despair at this point. We're here and we have to make the best of it. I, for one, am going to make the most of a good night's sleep while I can still get one," said Jamie, his usual kind smile on his face, but it dropped as he turned to walk into the tent, leaving the rest of them in silence.

Tristan looked into the flames jumping between each other and dancing up into the night's sky. This had certainly not been what he had expected when he'd been shuffled into the church in what seemed like a lifetime away. Now he was here, and most people seemed to be taking a very grim perspective on the whole thing. Yet he didn't quite know what to think about it all. He felt confused and not at all like the hero he hoped he would be. But there was still time to find his courage, he supposed, and part of that was over-coming the fear. But his fear seemed like a deep well in his gut, swirling downwards onto an abyss that made up his stomach. He did not want to die tomorrow or the next day, or really ever. All the men around them looked like they were already dead, their faces set and eyes shallow, but he couldn't bring himself to be like them.

When he eventually went to the tent to get some sleep, he closed his eyes to the thoughts of his refusal to die. He would see his grandparents again. He would see Isabella. He would get Joshua back to his wife. He simply had to, because he really didn't know what would happen if he didn't.

* * *

"THEY'RE COMING! Get out of your beds! Now soldiers!" ordered Ulysses waking Tristan with a jolt.

The light from outside was barely creeping in through the gap in the tent door. As Tristan sat up, he noted that he wasn't the only one to have been so rudely awakened, as the other men around him were blinking themselves awake. He quickly got out of bed, throwing on his chain shirt as quickly as he could, still hearing the voice of Ulysses booming through the camp. He tucked the long dagger behind his belt, placed the oversized helmet on his head, and scrambled out the tent grabbing his shield and axe on the way. Everything seemed to weigh more that morning, but he didn't have much time to dwell on the weight as he and the other men emerged, their faces mirroring the remains of last night's fire, dank and miserable.

The sun was barely in the sky when they exited the tent in a hurry, Ulysses on his white horse, shouting as he moved through the camp of the hundred men under his charge, four other mounted soldiers around him, echoing his shouts. The men were quickly directed to get to outside the camp on the road and wait for further instructions. Tristan ran with the other men, looking around in an attempt to see any signs of the enemy or clashing, but all he saw was the camp ahead of them, also forming into ranks and the camp behind them following close behind. He had to fully turn his head to see anything because his helmet bounced around on his head. When they got to the road, they began to form themselves, or attempt to form themselves, into ranks of ten like they had been marching in, but due to some unhappy shouting from Ulysses, they stopped doing anything until he gathered the rest of them.

"Spears at the front! Two ranks of spears!" he commanded at the top of his lungs, turning his horse back and forward indicating the length he wished the rank to be.

Tristan looked up to see Joshua making his way forward, but he was gone before Tristan could say anything to stop him. The ranks were now much wider than how they'd been marching and as Ulysses and his four mounted soldiers led them forward to the plains in front of them dotted by trees, Tristan could feel the well of fear getting deeper. Tristan was as near the middle of the ranks as anyone could be and so he simply walked the direction that everyone else did, not really seeing where they were heading, except that it was at a right angle.

When the three ranks of men came to a stop, it was in front of an almost barren field, with the odd tree and bush standing in the open. The morning mist still hovered and covered much of what Tristan was attempting to see. All he could note was that the unlevel ground seemed to sloping upwards but the mist obscured the ground.

Then they waited. Tristan didn't really know how long they waited. This was strange because he felt every single second of it. The men began to stir a little and even the horses began to fidget. The sun began to climb in the sky, and Tristan could feel the beads of sweat dripping down his face, two men he'd never met at his shoulders. He didn't know them, but he knew the look on their face well. He'd come to know what fear looked like.

Soon the mist began to rise from the incline, and that's when Tristan saw it, the sun reflecting from some armour. Apparently, he wasn't the only one to see it and those in front of the ranks began steadying their men. Then out of the mist from what still seemed a long way off, rode their enemy, and it sent shocks down Tristan's spine.

The men before them seemed much more than simply ravagers; they were knights, in heavy armour of steel shining in the cold sun, their lances pointed upwards as they rode together. Their horses were the largest Tristan had ever seen, each one even larger than the one Ulysses was riding, their own armour as polished as their riders. They wore white banners with a golden lamb on them, each individual Knight seeming to have slightly different imagery, but they all were in white. Their riding, even at a measured pace rattled Tristan to the bones, and this only increased as Ulysses' face turned white and he rode to the left flank with great haste.

When he returned his face was scarlet. He rode up to one of his soldiers and said something in his ear. That soldier pushed his horse passed the ranks and rode away down the path as quick as though wolves were on his tail. Ulysses then jumped off his horse and stood before his men, taking a swig from his flask.

"It is time men - death and honour be with you. Keep close ranks and try and take out the horses. Make the riders stuck. For the King!" he shouted.

He drew his sword, and the men around Tristan gave up a mighty shout to the point that he himself found that he, too, was screaming alongside them. Ulysses then made his way into the ranks and he disappeared from view. Tristan held his shield tight to him, trying to remember everything Joshua had taught him.

The hoard of white rode towards them, and from behind them more horses came. This time they had no armour and their riders were wearing leathers for armour. These men came from either flank, their horses swift and their axes keen. Yet they held their ground. Even though everything within Tristan wanted to turn and flee, he held his ground and his eyes up.

They came closer and closer, increasing with speed in every stride forward, their lances lowering in front of them. That's when they hit.

Tristan heard the screams and the shattered wood as the huge horses rode directly into their front ranks, not seeming to care for the spears that were held up to them. All they did was continue to push through them. Soon they were upon him, and didn't have enough time to worry about anyone else, as a horse came rushing past him, and as he lifted his shield, he heard the clash of metal against it. The force of the blow made him stumble backwards, but he caught himself again, nearly being hit by another grand horse that strode around him.

He looked around him. All that came to his eyes was blood and chaos, with dead men crushed into the ground by horses, their eyes in death still staring. Around him the horses were running through the men like butter, a couple of them being closed round by groups of men, their weapons hitting into the horse, bringing it down, dragging off the rider.

"Get down, fool!" screamed a voice and he felt himself being pushed out the way as a horse rushed by, and he then heard a shout of pain.

He looked round to see Ulysses clutching his shoulder, his turning red under it, his sword in his hand. Tristan tried to say something, but the words didn't come out. Ulysses quickly turned back around and tried to thrust his blade into another approaching horse. Tristan also tried to hit it as it went past, but the axe flew out his hand as he did so. Now all he could do was pull the long dagger from behind his back and follow Ulysses as he cut his way through the field, his hand on his shoulder and screaming orders at the men still on their feet. All the while, Tristan's heart was racing through his chest.

He had to dodge left and right to avoid the horses running through the men, their screams filling the air around them. Tristan tried to stab out at the horses running around him, but he really doubted he actually made an impact on the enemy, but it didn't stop him attempting. He felt so small seeing the knights riding through the ranks slashing at the men as they went down.

Tristan kept his shield high as he attempted to navigate his way through the bodies that were on the floor. Suddenly a slash hit the shield and it pushed him backwards, the shield spinning from his hand. He fell onto something soft, which he quickly attempted to leap off, his hand in his dagger. He looked down to see what he'd fallen on and he nearly threw up, when he saw Jamie lying there, a slash running through his chest.

He forced himself to turn away from it, tears running down his face as he looked up to witness a sword being thrust through the chest of Ulysses by a knight whose horse was rearing up. Tristan ran towards him, leaping over the bodies and horses, to get to the man who hit the ground, and the Knight rode away as if it were of no consequence. Tristan got to his side and all the man was able to was thrust his sword into Tristan's hand, and then he breathed his last.

Tristan knew that he had to pull himself up, but his entire body felt heavy underneath his chainmail and his arms now with a weapon in each hand felt paralysed. But he made himself stand up and look around, the sword in his hand already blood stained, as he lifted it into guard position. The majority of the knights had gone to the left flank, mercilessly tearing through the other men, but he saw an armoured man trying to get to his feet. His white markers were now brown and red, his sword red with the blood of the men Tristan had stood with.

This man got to his feet and tore off his helmet, his long brown hair robed with sweat. He looked exhausted, holding his sword loosely in one hand as he looked around him, and then he saw someone else, and his eyes locked onto him. Tristan followed them to see Joshua hacking into another downed knight, his sword in both hands, but his eyes meeting the other man.

Tristan forced himself to edge forward towards the man with the long hair, now holding his sword tighter in his gauntlet. Joshua didn't even take a moment to breathe after he downed the other man, his curved sword was in both his hands and he ran towards the knight. Tristan started into a jog keeping his eye on the men, then they clashed.

Joshua hit the other's sword out of the way and hit him square in the chest pushing him backwards, the armour taking much of the blow. The knight swiftly recovered, cutting twice in Joshua's direction, both blows had more force behind them than Tristan could think the tired man had within him, and Joshua took one of the blows on the leg.

Now Tristan was sprinting, his sword and dagger both gripped in his hands, as the knight now pushed and pushed again at Joshua. Although his leg was injured, Joshua was still quick and he dodged as many of them as he could, deflecting as many as he could with his blade and attempting to put in a few of his own, but the armour stayed true and all it did was make the man grunt.

Finally, one of the blows caught Joshua's side and he fell, then the knight was upon him, lifting up his sword to thrust down onto the other man. That was when Tristan thrust his blade into his exposed jaw, pushing it all the way into his head. The man fell back dead. He had killed someone. Tristan threw up everything he had left in his stomach, which was simply white liquid at this point.

"Thank you, Tristan," panted Joshua getting to his feet, still bleeding from his wounds.

"I mean to keep my promise," Tristan replied looking around at the battle which was still going on, albeit one-sided.

"You certainly did. Let's get out of here, there will be no one who will miss us," said Joshua moving forward, just very slowly, wincing as he did.

"What about everyone else?" asked Tristan.

He moved to help him, pulling his arm over his shoulder after he sheathed his dagger.

"I plan on keeping my end of the promise," replied Joshua.

Tristan made no complaint. He wanted to run with every part of his being, leaving the dreadful field behind them as soon as they could. The two men navigated their way through the battlefield, until they got to the road that they had camped next to. The camp was now destroyed, evidently by those who saw the battle was a victory and decided that they would pillage the campsite before the rest were done killing. The two men made their way through the remains attempting to salvage what they could for the journey home, until Joshua pointed out something in the trees. Tristan looked to see Ulysses' white horse, eating some grass behind the treeline. They hobbled to it and after a little pursuing, both got onto its back, and rode away.

Tristan wasn't particularly familiar with horses, but he made it ride as quickly as he could, putting as much distance between himself and the battlefield. He didn't care that this was not the action of a hero; he had seen death and he never wanted to see that again. The images of the battle were still twirling round his head, as they rode on into the day, putting as many miles as the horse could between them and the field of death.

# CHAPTER 11

## TALKS WITH THE ENEMY

he Smiling Duck was beginning to empty as all those whom Jacklin considered to be able-bodied men filed out of the tavern in twos and threes, making quiet conversation. Pip was left looking at the sketch of the town that they had used to plan for the next day, but his mind seemed not to be on what they had said in the meeting. Plans were all well and good until things get messy, then the first thing to die was the plan, no matter how simple it was. He cared more about the men that had now left, the tavern closing the door behind them, leaving him by himself in the main room. None of them had wielded a weapon before, never mind used one against someone. The only one of them he could properly rely on was the blacksmith named Carlos, who had enough muscle so that most things he hit would be at least damaged. He couldn't say the same for the other men.

The plan had revolved around the idea that Little Carr's buildings had very flat rooves, that Pip had the possibility of stalking across them to attempt to get a clear crossbow shot at the mage. There were a lot of moving pieces with the plan, and it relied on the town stead still being in one piece while it happened. Pip knew if he could kill the mage, the rest would be comparatively easily. The problem was if he missed a lot of good people could suffer.

"How did the planning go?" asked Jacklin walking out the kitchen.

Her apron as stained as usual, but her face was more concerned than interested. He hadn't quite known what he thought about her when he first met her, but he had grown to respect the way she could take charge of situations and the fact remained, she was the one who suggested this meeting in the first place.

"Well enough," Pip muttered.

He looked up for a moment to see her move to the other side of the table, but then just as suddenly looked down. He knew people would die tomorrow, they always did, but how many he couldn't be sure.

"In that case, you should get some sleep. You'll need all the energy you can get for tomorrow. And before you object, this is my Tavern, I will clear everything away," she insisted pointing to the room that he had been given to sleep in.

He didn't have it in him to argue back, so he made his way slowly up the stairs, only looking back when he got to the top to see that she had already got to work, cleaning the tables and mugs they had been using. The room he'd been staying in was not large; he had insisted on that when Jacklin and Peter had tried to get him into one of the bigger rooms. He didn't need more than what he had there, and he could have done without a lot of it. The room was dark when he came in, but his eyes adjusted quickly to see everything the way he had left it, apart from one thing - a letter left on the pillow of the bed.

He walked over to it, feeling the handle of the long dagger

behind his back out of instinct and his foot kicking the weapons under his bed to make sure they were still there. The hardness that met his boot at least confirmed something was there. This meant that whoever had been in his room had either not taken anything or replaced the weapons there with something of a similar make. He reached the letter and opened it carefully. There wasn't much to it, just a single piece of fine paper folded into an envelope. Tristan moved to the window so the light from the moon could illuminate the words scribbled on the paper.

*I would very much like to speak with you. I promise I will make it worth your while. Look for our camp off the road. Come alone.*

He read over it twice to try and get all the details. He then stuffed the letter into his belt and pulled the weapons from their place under the bed. He selected two throwing daggers to put in his boots, took the throwing axe and put it into his belt, he then took the buckler and strapped it to his arm. Finally, he pulled his dark green cloak around him. He doubted he was going to get any sleep that night, but that wouldn't be a huge change for him.

He listened to his door and heard the sound of Jacklin humming to herself as she went up the stairs, sweeping as she went. Pip decided that it would be easier to go out the window, so he took the rope from one of his packs, put it round his belt and opened the window. The night was a cool one and the stars were in all their glory were shining down upon the small-town stead. Pip wasn't one for stopping too long to admire anything, so he quickly got to work tying the rope to the bed and lowering himself down the building. Leaving the rope hanging out the window was a risk he would just have to take, as he needed a way back that he could make use of quickly if he was followed back.

Pip took one last glance at the room he'd just left and then went into the night, easily hopping the fence that surrounded the yard behind the Smiling Duck. Although he wasn't walking very stealthily, he wanted to remain unseen by those from the town stead. Seeing the man that you are expecting to save you running away could end hope and start rumours; neither would be helpful. He kept to the shadows where he could, but most of the way through the town, he simply kept his head down and keeping to a quick jog. At this hour of the night, most of the inhabitants would be asleep but taking unnecessary risks wasn't something he liked to do when he was already taking an unnecessary risk.

When he got to the edge of town stead, he made sure that he wasn't being followed and then disappeared into the night. He ran swiftly down the path towards the woods, his eyes constantly attempting to adjust to the darkness, but he knew the way well enough just from the feel of the dirt underneath his feet. When he got to the treeline, he slowed himself down to a swift walk, keeping his cloak wrapped around him. The trees were merely darker shadows at this point in the night and they blocked out the light of the moon. He moved forward, keeping to the right of the road keeping his eyes upwards, scanning the forest for any kind of noise or light that might give away people.

He didn't have to look for long as the sounds of laughter and drunkenness came to his ears from the left side of the trees. Pip stalked forward toward the sounds, moving from tree to tree, keeping out of sight. He eventually began to see firelight glowing from between the trees. Usually the light would come from to the eye first, but the trees were so tightly together that all he could see were two separate glowing fires. The furthest one was the source of the noise, and Pip could see shadows passing forward and back from in front of it. The other, a significantly smaller fire, was a little further away and there were no sounds coming from it at all.

Pip made his way towards the silent one staying as low as

he could, keeping his eye on the source of the noises. As he came closer, he heard the sounds of coarse laughter and singing, and every man that he could see through the trees had some kind of bottle or mug in their hands. He doubted that they would even hear him if he walked normally and upright, but he didn't want to take any chances. Taking too many of those could make you a dead man.

When he got nearer to the small fire, he kept the trees between himself and the fire, only making small movements to dart from tree to tree. As he got closer, his small glances between trees, he made out a man sitting alone at the fire on a fallen tree, his feet up on it and his eyes focused on the book he held in front of him. He had sharp features, with little facial hair that ran down his chin into a point. His eyes were small but sharp, and they were constantly running up and down the pages which turned at a surprising rate. Pip got to almost a step away from being in the firelight, keeping his eyes on the man, but he just continued as he did before.

"Please come in, just allow me to finish this page," said the man not looking up from his book once.

Pip knew that it wasn't worth waiting for him to ask twice, so he walked in, scanning for guards of any kind. People who had to ask twice often got impatient, and then they gave away less, and he wanted some answers. The voice did match the one from the masked man from the morning, but it was significantly less deep and booming.

"Thank you for coming, I'm so glad you came. Please do take a seat," he smiled closing his book and spinning himself round to face Pip properly.

He was by no means a strong man; his body resembled that of a twig than a man, but his eyes were keen and danger-ous. Pip positioned himself to the other side of the fallen tree, leaning on it rather than sitting properly, always ready to push himself off it in case something happened.

"Do you care for some wine? Don't worry it's not poisoned. If I wanted you dead, I would've killed you this morning," he offered walking over to a small tent at the edge of the fire and pulling out two goblets and a green bottle.

"I assumed that when you didn't aim that fireball at me," replied Pip watching the man carefully as he poured the red liquid in the bottle into the goblets.

He then approached offering both goblets to Pip, who choose one, but waited for the other man to drink before he took a sip. He couldn't be too careful. The wine was good, which added further to the questions he had for the man who was now resuming his seat on the tree.

"So, you can talk - that's a good start. You didn't seem very fazed by the little display that I put on; you were the only person in the entirety of the town without a pale face. Even my own men get skittish when I do things like that," he said gesturing to the other fire and for a moment Pip could hear breaking glass and then more laughter, to which the man in front of him rolled his eyes taking a deep drink from the goblet.

"I've seen worse," replied Pip.

He brought the goblet to his lips but only feigned drinking the liquid. Losing his edge was a foolish thing to do, and he could be called many things, but a fool wasn't one of them.

"You've seen a lot of the world, that's good to hear. Very good indeed. I do, however, have to ask, what is a sell sword of your proficiency doing in a barely developing town stead like Little Carr? Do they have some vast hoard of gold they've hidden from us? I promise you however much they've promised you, I'd give you more," said the man calmly taking another hearty swig from the goblet.

He kept his eyes on Pip the entire time. They were the

eyes of a dangerous man, a man who wouldn't stop at much for the sake of gain.

"I'm not a sell sword and I'm not doing it for any money," Pip replied, maintaining the eye contact, but not allowing himself to ease.

"My apologies, you're their hero. Their restorer of hope and the like," said the man gesturing with his hand in the air, his shadows rising high behind him as he did so, as if it were another creature.

"I'm not a hero."

"Well that gives me hope. The name's Mortimer by the way in case you wanted it. You see…"

"Pip."

"You see, Pip, I'm not here just to take already poor people's possessions, I have a grander purpose, it's why we wear the masks, see. I have very powerful people above me, people who are looking for loyalty and potential," he began.

Continuing he said, "Well, striking fear into people's hearts in small town steads in Libarantor is simply the beginning, I've been promised power beyond imagination. You see the men over there, they're just some ruffians I picked up along the way, with the promise of gold. In exchange, they wore masks, but what I need is loyalty to me and skills. Skills that you possess."

"So, the reason I asked you to come is that I could use a man like you on my way up. It also seemed a shame to kill someone with such potential as you have. The people above me would see you as a most valued asset. You could be rich or powerful. What do you say to that?" asked Mortimer, his arms taking on a life of their own as he described his offer and the shadow behind him seemed even more animated than the man, the flames dancing in his eyes.

When he'd finished, Pip looked into his goblet for a

moment, but then turned to see the hopeful yet greedy eyes of the man looking back at him.

"Since when did the Bloodspire council use novice mages to spread fear?" Pip asked, and the blood drained from Mortimer's face, and even his shadow got smaller behind him.

"How do you know about them?"

"I know a lot. More than you may think. You asked me what I was doing in the town stead. I came because of you. I know the description of the Phantoms of Shadow when I hear it," he said his voice level as he always tried to maintain it, but he wished he could scream at the man.

"No one is supposed to know that name yet! You came for us? Why?" said Mortimer attempting to adjust himself on his sitting position, but there was still no blood in his face.

"I came because of a simple reason - revenge. The people above you hurt a friend of mine, and now I might get the tiniest piece of satisfaction by killing you. You and every one of your men."

Pip maintained his eye contact with the man, but his hand was on his long dagger the entire time, just waiting for the other man to think about moving his hands or saying a word of power.

"So, you're a good man? Looking for revenge for a friend? It's sweet, it really is, but I don't think you know who you're really dealing with here. You may have read books about the things you've said, but the real thing would make your nightmares look like a picnic. I serve them, and I have done it well, and I will enjoy killing you tomorrow," shouted the man, and from the other campfire, there was some commotion as a reaction to the outburst.

"I'm not a good man. You better thank the heavens that I'm not. Because when a good man thrusts a sword through their chest and you look them in the eye, you will see right-eous anger, and you will die knowing that whatever you did was so bad, you made a good man take your life. I'm not a good man. When I put my blade into your chest, you will look into my eyes and only see pain," Pip said standing up and walking towards the man.

Mortimer screamed, bringing his hands up and opening his mouth. But, before any words came out Pip had thrust his long dagger into his chest looking him dead in the eye. The man looked down at the blade now stuck in him and then looked up at Pip, a look of almost surprise that someone would have the audacity to do such a thing. But all Pip did was look at him until his eyes went dull, and then retrieved his dagger.

The sounds of the other men came closer as they came to investigate why their leader had screamed and whether they were needed and Pip decided this would be the best time to leave. He leapt over the fallen tree and ran into the wood, weaving swiftly through the woods as he did so, not really caring about the noise he was making as he did so. Some-times plans changed. He had got rid of the man who would have caused the most death to Little Carr. However, the night was far from over and he knew it.

Pip pushed as fast as he could into the forest, jumping past trees and over roots, always rearing to the left in an attempt get back onto the path. He couldn't hear the sounds of his pursuers yet, but he knew they would be coming. No matter how skilled of warrior he was, he knew where his limits lay; seven men would be too much for him, especially in a group. For a moment as he pushed past another tree, he considered picking them off one by one using the darkness of the forest for cover, but he knew better than that. They weren't chasing after him, so to speak, they were going to make the innocent people of Little Carr pay for their sudden lack of leadership and source of payment. Good people might die, but if he stayed alive, he knew that fewer would. Maybe this was the night for him to die, maybe it wasn't, but he needed to have breath in his lungs long enough to see the last of the masked men die.

He saw the path coming towards him and he pushed himself to make his legs go faster. Every second he was ahead of them was a second that Little Carr had to prepare for what was about to happen to them. He had taken out the largest chance of them all being burnt alive, even a novice in the ways of the arcane could do that, but now he had bought a real chance of victory. And with every second he put between him and his pursuers, he bought them more hope.

When Pip got to the path, he leapt onto it, and kept on running. He could feel his body begging to stop being pushed; he wasn't as young as he used to be, but he refused to yield. Gritting his teeth, he focused on toward the odd shaped shadows ahead of him and the occasional lamp still left lit. He was so close. He imagined he could hear the voices and the sounds of pursuers behind him and he took it as the motivation he needed to run into the town stead.

"We are under attack!" he shouted using all the breath left in his lungs to scream into the silence of the night.

There was no response, just silence. Pip tried to shout again but all his lungs could do was take in air. He looked over to the forest he had ran out of and he could swear he saw shadows moving around and white blurs cutting through the night. He made himself stand up straight, drawing his sword calmly and taking his throwing axe in the other. At least he would die before anyone else had to. He'd watched a lot of people die, but he wasn't sure if he could live through watching all of these innocent people die.

Then the bells from the church tower began to chime. Again and again, until the silence was filled with the sounds of ringing. That's when lights started turning on and the blinds began to be opened. For the first time in a while, he felt a swelling in his heart. He believed that was what hope felt like. He would not die alone that night.

# CHAPTER 12

## THE LONG ROAD HOME

*E*very time Tristan closed his eyes, all he could see were the faces and bodies of the dead. His dreams were full of them, calling out to him to save them, to do something for them, but he could do nothing. All he could do was stare horrified into their lifeless eyes and weep. Then he'd wake up in a cold sweat, sometimes he would scream, other times he would be panting as if he'd run a great distance. All he hoped was that every morning he would forget, but they remained just as vivid, just as bloody, every time he shut his eyes.

Joshua and he had been on the road for a week now, taking country lanes in an attempt to make their way back home the quickest and safest route possible. Joshua's injuries to his legs meant that he could only hobble around instead of walking which meant that he was the one riding the horse although he didn't seem happy about it. They didn't talk a lot as they travelled; Tristan didn't know what to say apart from the odd observation and odd reply. He didn't feel much like talking. They simply went along in silence to the sound of the horse's hooves and Tristan's boots on the dirt roads.

The days would have been considered lovely as the sun was set in an azure blue sky which kept them warm, but there was also a gentle breeze that kept them from being too hot. The scenery was also idyllic with the dirt road passing through patches of woodland and little streams that gurgled their way happily beside the road. The birds were plentiful and made their usual playful music as they danced in the air. When they made camp at night, they didn't have to go far to find water or hunt too long to find roots or rabbits that they could use for food. Yet to Tristan it all seemed dull, unreal, like the monotony of walking every day was the dream, and the nightmares that woke him up were his true reality. Even the blisters on his feet didn't feel as painful as they should; they just felt numb.

On the seventh day of walking, they made camp near a small river. The water was cool and what both men needed after their day of walking; even the horse looked happy. After they'd refilled their canteens, Tristan took off his boots and dipped his raw feet in the cool water, and simply sat in the sun for a while. Even Joshua hobbled to the edge of the river and sat his back to a tree taking in the sunlight. His walking was becoming steadier, but he stilled winced every time he stood up and sat down, and this time was no different. Tristan watched the sun rays flood through the trees and onto the dark water that flowed by, yet when he closed his eyes to try and simply enjoy the warmth on his face, the dead returned.

"How did you live with it?" he asked abruptly, still looking at the river rather than at Joshua, watching it flow and splash against rocks that stuck their heads above the water level.

"Live with what?" Joshua asked, his voice steady, but with a hint of softness to it that was new to Tristan.

"You talked about dragon fire and watching men die.

How do you live after seeing something like that?" he choked, his voice breaking slightly in the middle, but he put that more down to growing up than the tears rolling down his face.

"You don't really live with it; you simply exist with the memories in your head. I had to live my life after seeing my father consumed by dragon fire in front of me, and every night I closed my eyes, I saw his face just before the torrent of fire came. I even see it now sometimes," Joshua replied, wincing as he got to his feet, but his voice maintained its softness.

"I don't want to live with it all still in my head. I don't want to think of a life where I wake up every day knowing that if I shut my eyes, I will see those same men dead in front of me. I will see the same man I put my sword through his skull. I just don't," Tristan said. He tried with everything he had to keep his voice steady, but in the end, he burst into tears. He held his face in his hands, until he felt Joshua sitting himself next to him.

"I'm sorry," he sobbed.

First he was a coward for running and now he was simply a stupid boy crying in front of a real soldier.

"You never have to apologise for you crying. Never. Every man cope with the pain in some way. Some drink, some keep on killing for the rest of their lives and others cry. Crying is the best of the three, and never something to be ashamed of," said Joshua gently.

He placed his hand on Tristan's chin to look him in the eye, and through the tears Tristan could see the intense seriousness in his eyes, but also a deep softness in them. He then pulled him into his chest and let him cry. Tristan cried until he had no tears left, and then tried to cry more. His eyes were sore, and his nose was wet, but he still tried to cry more. There was a constant lump in his belly that didn't feel as bad when he cried, so he almost tried to force himself to cry more. But he knew his tears were spent so he pulled himself up and rubbing his nose with his sleeve.

"Which one did you do to cope?" he asked still sniffing the liquid up from his nose.

"Well, I cried until I didn't have any tears left. Then I drank until I didn't have any money left. Then I decided to join the army again and was so good at it, I became a member of the elite guard. None that really helped me cope in the long term, but then I met Rosa. She made everything feel a lot better, and soon the nightmares stopped," Joshua replied looking forward into the river, his face smiling when he mentioned Rosa.

"So, you fell in love?" asked Tristan looking up at Joshua smiling a little, still wiping the tears from his eyes.

"Essentially," smiled Joshua looking back at Tristan, and then pulled himself up wincing as he did so his wounds were still healing.

"So, what should I do then? Fall in love?" laughed Tristan looking up at him, a real smile coming across his face.

"I think you should make dinner," smiled Joshua and then hobbled towards the camp, still smiling as he did so.

Tristan waited for a moment, still looking forward at the river, closing his eyes to soaking the warmth for a little while longer. As he did so, the images flashed through his head, but they were vaguer and faster. Maybe the crying had helped little. He took a deep breath and then pushed himself up, making his way slowly towards Joshua who was busy feeding the horse and stroking his face tenderly.

After their meal that evening, Joshua insisted on running him through some drills with his sword, particularly the correct way to thrust with the thin blade. Every time he ran through the exercise, he couldn't help but see the man after he had put the sword through his head, his eyes shocked open as the body hit the ground, his own sword falling out his limp hands. Yet he gritted his teeth and continued with it, and every time he did it, the image became fainter, his muscles getting used to the correct lunging motion that Joshua insisted upon. By the time he got to bed, he was too tired to have thoughts before he slept. His feet were sore and his arms now matched them. He slept quickly, his blanket pulled around as he did so.

Apparently being tired didn't cause the nightmares to cease though, as he was still haunted by the images of the battlefield. But this time, there was less of a focus on the bodies on the floor but the battle horses speeding past him making him run and duck for cover. Every knight on the horse had the face of the man he had slain, and even when the horse had passed him the head turned unnaturally to stare into his soul. He ran as fast as he could away from the horse but everywhere he went they would appear out of seemingly nowhere. They closed in around him, the faces looming closer and closer, their shocked eyes now bleeding.

He woke up screaming, beads of sweat dripping down his face. Tristan looked about himself to see Joshua packing away the rest of their camp, simply looking at him with the eyes that were soft as pillows yet as hard as stone. Tristan used his sleeve to try and rub away the sweat as he stood up to stretch his muscles. The sun was out again that morning, but the breeze was a little bit colder than the day before, cutting into him a little.

"I think we're a day away from home," observed Joshua trying not to hobble as he put the last of the packs onto the horse.

"That's good to hear; it'll be nice to be home," replied Tristan.

He walked towards the river, but stopped to smile for a moment as he thought of his grandparents, home-made food, a soft bed and Isabella. He put his hand in his pocket and the necklace she'd given him was still there, and that made him smile more.

"I figure we'll get to your farm a few hours after midday, then I can go onto home from there," said Joshua raising his voice so that Tristan could he hear him as he splashed water onto his face and torso.

"We can go to your farm first; you're barely in a state to walk to the house and I doubt Rosa will be able to help you much. Anyway, I have a promise to keep to you, to get you home safely," smiled Tristan. Still he could see his nightmares vividly every time he shut his eyes to splash water on his face.

"Well, we'll see how it goes, Tristan. I imagine if your grandparents see you walking past their house, they won't be able to contain themselves and you may be forced to let me ride home," said Joshua getting onto the horse, wincing with every movement he made, but he was soon on the beast and ready to be moving.

"That's true- we'll just have to be extra careful," said Tristan walking back into the camp, readying himself for the last leg of their journey.

This wasn't how he had envisaged his return home from his adventure, if adventure you could call it.

After pulling his boots on and getting his pack ready, the two men were off in their usual fashion, making little to no conversation. Tristan didn't think he recognised much of the terrain around them, but he had to admit there was something familiar about the fields that the road ran past. As the day wore on, the sun began to climb higher but the wind remained cold, forcing the two men put on their cloaks for protection from the wind. There were even clouds that occasionally covered the sun, making it both cold and breezy, yet these clouds were infrequent and they'd soon receive a pleasant amount of light. They didn't hear the usual sounds of birds. All they heard was the sounds of boots and hooves.

The road they were following came to a crossroads and Joshua instructed that they should turn to the left. As they continued to walk, eating their midday meal on the go, Tristan found that bits and pieces of the countryside were familiar to him. There were fields he'd always looked on from different angles and patches of trees that were up close that he'd usually see from a distance. He even found himself walking a little faster, the hope of home at the front of his mind as he did so.

Almost out of nowhere, they emerged from some trees, and there stood his grandparent's farm, unchanged from the day he left it. He couldn't stop himself letting go of the reins and running to it, he was so happy to be back. He stood in front of it all, taking in the sight of the farmhouse and the barn, things that he'd missed seeing every day. There were the fences that were part broken that his grandfather always insisted he would fix but never did. There was the smell of animals that filled his lungs. But something seemed off. The smell of the animals would always be mixed with the smell of his grandmother's fresh cooking, yet the cooking smell was not there. Something was wrong.

He leapt over the fence and barged into the house, but it was empty and completely lifeless. Everything seemed the same, the table and chairs were still upright, many of the pans were still there and there was even dried food in the cupboards. It wasn't right.

"What's the matter?" asked Joshua as Tristan left the farmhouse slamming the door behind him, confusion and frustration setting in.

"I don't know, but something isn't right," he murmured.

His eyebrows were knitted together trying to think of a reason why his grandparents would not be in their house.

They were older now, so travelling would be out of the question. It didn't look like anyone had tried to force an entry. It was perplexing, and it also didn't help that his thought processes were confused by the images of his nightmares.

"In that case, we should get to my house as quick as we can," said Joshua as Tristan leapt back over the fence, his hand making its way to the sword at his side, his face losing all its softness. It was now set in grim determination.

They made their way down the lane towards the McArthur farm, both men with their hands on their swords and constantly scanning the road for anything that might attempt to take them by surprise. The sky became greyer as it filled with clouds, blocking any warmth from the sun. The wind began to pick up and the trees around them rustled with a fury. There was something haunting about the road that Tristan had been so used to walking down. Something was not right.

They soon got to the road that led off into the McArthur's farmhouse and Joshua stopped the horse, looking at his home for a moment. He then swung his leg over the saddle with a great wince and came off the horse. Tristan came to his side quickly, steadying him as he got used to the ground for a moment.

"You're in no state to walk," he commented as Joshua attempted to hobble a few steps wincing a little as he did so.

"I want to be able to look my wife in the eye when I see her; I can't do that from a horse," Joshua replied continuing his hobble towards the farmhouse.

"Then we'll do it together," insisted Tristan.

He put the man's arm over his shoulder, and held the horses' reins in the other hand. Joshua gave him a small smile, but quickly turned back to walking as fast as he was able towards the building. Tristan kept him upright and also attempted to match his pace, which was difficult with the weight of the man on his shoulders. He looked about him at those that trees he had hidden in that night before they left and at the large pond. It all seemed grey against the cloudy sky; even the leaves looked duller.

As they approached the house, they heard a commotion coming from inside, and the door flung open and a weeping Rosa ran out her arms opened wide. She was as beautiful as she always was, but she has seemed to have put on a little weight in the stomach, but Tristan wouldn't be so rude to mention such a thing. Joshua let go of him and hobbled to his wife, and they met in an embrace. Tristan decided it was better for him to observe the sky for a moment as husband and wife reunited. They took their time in reuniting, and if it wasn't for his worry for his grandparents, Tristan would have been quite bored looking at the grey clouds.

"You're back so soon and you're injured, please come in," said Rosa after their reunion was complete and Tristan felt he could look again..

"I'm only back because of Tristan; he saved my life and got me back home," smiled Joshua, looking back to where Tristan was standing with the horse, and all he could think to do was give an awkward wave.

"My many thanks Tristan for saving my husband's life. I do not know what I could do to repay you. If we have a son, he will have your name," she smiled referencing her stomach, her eyes brighter from her joy, and all Tristan could do was smile politely while inwardly blushing. Pregnant, of course, she was pregnant. He felt like such a fool. So much for his theories about stomach-ache or gaining weight.

"You don't need to do that at all, I didn't do much. One thing you could help me with is tell me where my grandparents are. We went past the farm and there wasn't anyone there, it looked abandoned," said Tristan looking at the beaming couple still in each other's arms.

"I'm so sorry, I should've said this when you first came, but I was so happy. There were rumours of bandits in the area, and since most of the men went to work, the farmers thought it prudent to move to Tindale temporarily. So, your grandparents, the Harpers and many others were staying in Tindale for a couple of weeks, walking back home to feed livestock and such," she replied putting her hand to her chin.

"Well - I'll head to Tindale now then," said Tristan urgently.

He longed to see his grandparents and Isabella. He could still feel the necklace in his pocket and he touched it for a moment as he remembered her.

"You can't. It's not safe. There's been black smoke pouring out the village since not two days back; it only stopped this morning," explained Rosa her face falling, and Joshua held her closer to his chest.

Tristan said nothing for a moment. He couldn't think of what to feel or do. His grandparents, his best friend, Tindale - it could all be in danger.

"I need to go," he said quietly, mounting the horse hastily and pushed it forward, racing out and onto the lane.

He only barely heard Joshua shouting for him to wait and think, but neither were things that he wanted to do. He had to see his grandparents again. He had to see Isabella again. He had to.

He pushed the horse as fast as it could go. It was a horse used to long distances and being pushed, so it still had a lot of energy left in it. As he turned at the farm he had once called his home, he headed towards Tindale.

He set his face hard. The time for crying was over. He felt his insides becoming colder and number. He pushed the horse to move faster. As he approached towards Tindale, wisps of smoke rose up before him.

There was nothing left but rubble, broken wood and

black, burnt trees. Tristan paused for a moment to bring his white horse to a halt and gazed at it all, the numbness growing. He then continued to ride to the village. He needed to see them again. He needed to. Because if he didn't, he didn't know what he would do.

# CHAPTER 13

## FIRE AND SHADOW

*P*ip moved steadily backwards, his axe loose in his hand, but his sword tight, his eyes glued to the entrance of the village. They would be coming, and he was going to kill as many of them as he could. The street around him became lighter as people began hanging lanterns outside their houses. Men told their wives and children to go back inside their houses. Pip looked over his shoulder to see Peter coming out of his store, the sword that he had given him in his hand, fear written all over him. Pip couldn't help but smile at this. He wouldn't be a lot of use in a fight, but he admired the man's courage. Even Carlos stepped out of the smithy with a large black hammer in his hand, his sleeves rolled up to reveal his hairy arms.

The more men that came out with various assortments of kitchen knives and wood axes, the more light was being added to the street from lanterns and from the homes they'd emerged from. This resulted in the shadow in front of Pip becoming darker and darker. He could see nothing in it, and all he could hear was the sounds of the people murmuring in fear. Pip gritted teeth. He was never fond of not being able to see his enemy, but still, he readied himself.

That's when the white masks appeared in the darkness. Like ghosts, they floated in the darkness, slowly coming towards him. It was so dark, Pip couldn't see the faces of the bodies of the men wearing them, only the masks. Pip could smell death in the air, as the seven men stepped into the light, their black robes wrapped around them, their cruel weapons in their hands, ready for his blood. The people around him stepped back towards their porches trying to stay away from the phantoms that walked forward.

The man at the front of them held his mace towards Pip and shouted, "Now you die!"

It echoed through the town stead, making the men tremble, but it was all Pip needed. This would be it, either Little Carr would be free or it would be his day to die.

With a swift motion, he launched his throwing axe, and it embedded itself directly in the head of the one at their head, cracking the mask and staining it with blood. He fell backwards, his companions roared charging towards him, and Pip readied himself, his buckler forwards and his sword ready.

They all charged towards him in a group, but there were two that reached him first, the first of which brought a blow down to him which he deflected with the buckler, quickly jumping away as the second made his attack. He moved back thrusting where he could, but he was in the middle of the street and the four were coming to surround him. That was when he heard the mighty roar from Carlos making mighty swings at one to his left, pushing him out of the fray.

Pip moved swiftly, making sure to always have his back free by thrusting towards any of the five facing him that attempted to move behind him. They came at him, often in pairs, but he used the buckler effectively to take one attack and jump away from the other. He was moving as much as he could, striking out as much as he dared, yet they were closing in on him.

That was when Peter and three other men with axes jumped on two, distracting them for long enough for him to start taking risks with the other three. He drove forward towards the one to his left and deflected the odd blows from the other two who tried to close in. But they were too late. His blade thrust deeply into the man's chest, causing the body to go limp.

He didn't have time to celebrate, but quickly used his pressing momentum to leap over the railing of one of the houses. The two still at his tail made a wild swing, hitting his calf as leapt. The pain shot up his leg but he had no time to worry about that, as he grabbed a lantern hanging from the porch roof, and brought it down onto closest man's head, setting his robes ablaze.

The man engulfed in flames began screaming in pain, dropping on the floor to attempt to put out the fire. Pip used the opportunity to stray to the left, making faint attacks to the man in front of him as he did. The man followed him but swung wide in attempt to parry one of his faint thrusts, leaving his body exposed. Pip quickly cut down across his chest, a dash of blood out, but it had the desired effect. He fell backwards.

Pip walked down the porch pulling up his boot to himself, pulled the dagger he had there and threw it into the man in flames whose body was shaking around in pain, but as it hit him, it stopped. He then pushed his sword into the man, now on the floor moaning with pain, and he stopped his moaning.

He then looked up at the other skirmishes taking place. Carlos was holding his own against his opponent, beating him with his hammer. He turned to see the two other masked men, and he grimaced a little when he saw one of the men from Little Carr already on the floor, a wound on his head. The other two were attempting to stab at the other one, but they were being beaten back quickly. What really made Pip move quickly was seeing Peter being pushed back by one of the masked men with an axe. He managed to jump out the way, as many times as was possible, but he was slowing and that only encouraged his opponent to keep on cutting towards him.

Pip ran forward, keeping himself low, pulling the other knife from his boot. He saw the masked man knock down Peter with a jab from the axe head and was about to lift his axe up to finish the job, but Pip's knife embedded itself into his shoulder and pushed him off balance. Pip was then upon him and after two simple cuts, he was on the floor. He turned to Peter and pulled him up from the floor.

"Are you all right?" he asked turning towards the last man standing, who had already dropped another one of his attackers.

Peter nodded exhaustedly, and so Pip ran to his next opponent, his sword up and reflecting the firelight from the lanterns.

The masked man kicked the man from Little Carr forwards and brought up his mace ready to kill the man. Pip forced himself to run as fast his legs would take him, leaping in front of the man as the blow came down. He took it squarely on his shoulder and he could feel the bone underneath cracking, but he didn't have time for the pain as he thrust his on blade up the man's head. From inside the mask, he saw his eyes dilate and then the last breath of air left his lungs.

They stood for a moment like statues, the mace still in Pip's shoulder and his sword still up the other man's jaw. Then the masked man fell to the side, and his mace fell off

143

the shoulder, releasing the weight on it but making the pain worse. He gritted his teeth as he tried to move it, but instead a shot of pain ran from it and made him wince. His calf also began to properly start crying out in pain, and the little movement he could achieve was a limp. But Peter was soon at his side and the man put Pip's arm over his shoulder and pushed him upright. That's when he saw it.

Everyone in the town stead was there, all in various states of undress. But they were standing on their porches and even in the street, all looking at him. Apart from those attending the two men on the floor, they were smiling. Peter turned him around to get the full view of everyone, saw Father Michael who gave him a bow on his way round. Pip couldn't help look at the two men on the floor, two good men died, less than he'd feared but more than he'd hoped. Although their people were dead, it didn't stop the people around him from smiling.

They ended with looking up at Jacklin standing in front of the Smiling Duck, her eyes full of tears but her smile was so wide, she could be laughing. Maybe this is what hope looked like. Peter tried to move towards the Smiling Duck, but it became quickly apparent that he would not be able to shift the older man easily, but he didn't have to struggle for long as Carlos took over the job. The large man helped Pip limp to the tavern steps and then up them. Pip tried to smile at Jacklin as he went past her, but all he could manage was a wince.

Carlos helped him into the Tavern, but Jacklin quickly overtook them, guiding them to a bedroom on the ground floor. Pip didn't much to say on the matter, as they went into a corridor under the staircase and into a room that was too big for his taste. But it felt good to take the weight from his leg and shoulder as he was laid on the bed.

The pain was still there, overwhelming his senses. It was

an effort to keep his eyes open and his mind was barely aware of what came next. He thought he heard Jacklin giving orders to various people, and was vaguely aware of Carlos and Jacklin removing his armour. He remembered the pain when they got to his shoulder, but they only stopped for a moment before taking it fully off him. Pip also had a vague memory of Jacklin and another woman cleaning his wounds and then bandaging them up. While his was happening, he saw the figures of Peter with Amys in front of him, whispering something comforting, while Father Michael stood in front of the bed praying.

He couldn't remember falling asleep, but he did. The nightmares were always the same, the men he had killed coming back to haunt him. Their faces were vague and their eyes white, familiar faces in his dreams. This time the dream seemed much calmer and it ended with him simply being shallowed by darkness. He preferred it when his dreams were simply black, a rare occasion, when he would simply walk in the darkness, peacefully walking forward. At least he thought it was forward, the darkness was the same whichever way he moved, but within the dream it always felt like he was moving forward. The darkness was the last thing he saw before he awoke.

Pip's eyes opened slowly, blinking to adjust to the light around him produced from the two windows to his left where the light poured in. He lay in a bed that was large, with white sheets that matched the rest of the room's colour scheme. The room was long and a little wider than the bed, with dark wood furniture: a cupboard, a table with three finely made chairs around it. The fourth of the set was at the end of his bed, and there sat Jacklin busying herself with embroidery, her brown hair down and lip pursed in concentration on her work.

Pip tried to move himself from his bed but found that his

shoulder and leg were both stiff and still painful. He looked to his shoulder and saw that it had been properly bandaged up to support what he could only assume was a nasty bruise and a breakage. The motion made him wince with pain, his shoulder telling him that he still wasn't ready to move. It also alerted Jacklin to his consciousness, who put her embroidery down to look over to him.

"I'm glad to see that you're awake," she smiled, pulling her hair into a tight bun as she did so.

"People made talk about you not waking up again, but I knew it would take more than a broken shoulder and damaged calf to kill you."

"How long have I been sleeping?" asked Pip trying to take the tension from his injuries, but there was still a numb pain to them.

He could, of course, live with such pain, but he would still have to lie in the bed perhaps another day before he'd be able to walk about, and he hated not being able to do anything. Lying in bed was its own form of torture for him.

"Only fourteen hours. You really should've slept for longer; you'd be surprised what rest does for the healing process," she said standing up from her chair but staying at the end of the bed, her eyes on him, but with a kind smile on her face.

"What about the two men?" he asked trying to remember their faces.

If he forgot them, they died for nothing. He had to remember every good man that died on his watch to remind himself of what he was not.

"They died, I'm afraid. Father Michael held a service for them in the morning; the entire town stead came to show their respects. They were buried near the church, under the apple tree that grows behind the building. I think many consider them heroes," she pointed, moving slowly towards the door, but her eyes were still on him, and her face was still bright although she lowered her smile for talking about the dead.

"I'm glad they got a good funeral; I'm sure they were good men," he said quietly, looking up to the ceiling; they had to be better than he was, but that wasn't hard.

"Well - they weren't the only men from last night considered heroes, you know. And I'll give it to you, you killed them all. We're free now because of what you did for us. I'll be honest with you. When you first rode into town, I really didn't think you would be the man to put a stop to the masked men, but you really did come through with what you promised to do," she said opening the door.

But still she didn't walk through it; she was continued looking at him with a smile. It almost made him uncomfortable how much the woman was beaming at him.

"All I did was help," he shrugged, but the action made him wince a little due to the pain from his shoulder.

"Of course. Well, there's a lot of people who want to see you, but there's two in particular who are very anxious to see you."

And with that Amys burst into the room, quickly followed by Peter, also wearing smiles. Amys ran over to the bed immediately, and jumped onto it next to him, making him wince from the motion, but she was so excited that she didn't notice.

"You did it! You did it! You got rid of all the nasty men!" she exclaimed as she bounced up and down in pure excitement, and with every bounce, he winced a little.

Peter came behind her and put his hand on her shoulder to calm her down, and her bouncing slowing down.

"What I think she means to say is thank you," beamed Peter looking down at his daughter for a moment before he went back to smiling at Pip.

"Thank you," mumbled Amys, looking down sheepishly, but she soon resumed her bubbly personality.

"Thank you from all of us. Some of the other men and I went to the camp and recovered everything that was stolen from us. Everything is back where it belongs; we are no longer in fear of our lives, and that's all thanks to you. All I can say is thank you," he smiled still beaming as he did so, and Pip couldn't look too long.

All his smiling made him feel uncomfortable inside, like he was the reason for it all. It felt very strange to him.

"Well, Pip needs to get his rest. Let's give him the space he needs to get it," Jacklin said gesturing towards the door, still with her soft voice and disconcerting smile.

Amys took one more look at Pip, gave him a happy grin and then bounced off the bed, skipping her way to the door. Peter gave him another smile and followed his daughter out of the room.

"You know you flinch every time someone smiles at you," said Jacklin her smile increasing to a little chuckle.

"I'm just not used to it," he replied, trying to find a comfortable position in the bed, where both his shoulder and calf felt comfortable.

"Well, you may have to get used to it. You've given people hope - you might find yourself becoming a hero," she said walking out the room closing the door behind her, leaving Pip alone to his thoughts, his aching body and his pain.

He wasn't a hero. He knew that very well, however, the people in this town didn't know that. They didn't even know his real name, but even he forgot it sometimes. He knew he couldn't stay here for long; he had some unfinished business. Once his body healed and he was able to hold a sword, he knew what he had to do. His debt wasn't paid yet, and it would be one day, whether it was blood on his sword or with his dying breath. He would have his revenge.

# CHAPTER 14

## A PROMISE

*T*ristan rode into the smouldering ruins that was once the village of Tindale. The buildings that had once stood strong were now merely heaps of rubble, their roofs collapsed in on themselves from fire. Even the tree round which the entire village was built was burnt black with fire, no leaves left to show its vibrant life; now only bare branches. The church was the most consumed by the fire, its rubble closer to its foundations than any of the other buildings in Tindale.

Tristan lowered himself from the horse, drawing his sword as soon as his feet were on the ground. This was all wrong to him. Everything was burnt and destroyed, everything that he had hoped to come back to. Nothing was left but rubble and ashes.

Out of the corner of his eye, he saw some movement, and he turned quickly towards it, his sword pointed out between him and whatever it was. The numbness felt so all-consuming that he actually didn't think he would mind killing again.

The source of the movement was a man walking towards

him with his hands in the air attempting to approach him. He wore what could be described as fine clothes at one time, but they were blackened by fire and torn in many places. His face had a very fine beard, perhaps once well kept, but neglected somewhat over the past few days. His face also bore a raw patch of skin, down the entirety of the left side making one of his eyes squint.

"Who are you?" demanded Tristan bringing his blade up to the man.

His voice sounded harsh, but he didn't mind that. Coming across wrong was the least of his concerns at this moment in time.

"My name is Reuben; I am a simple merchant of dyes and other items that take people's fancy. Please lower your sword, can't you see I've suffered enough?" the man before him begged, gesturing to the raw skin on the side of his face.

For a moment Tristan let his blade go down as he looked at the man's face. He was clearly one of those of suffered from what happened here, but he quickly resumed his guarded position.

"What happened here?" again, Tristan demanded.

He was aware his voice was raised with all the emotion that was racing inside of his veins. Someone had to blame for this.

"Many awful things. Please put away the sword so we may speak like people rather than enemies," Reuben pleaded moving over to the base of the tree and lowering himself to sit.

Tristan looked the man over one more time and realised that he wouldn't do him any harm, so he sighed and sheathed his sword, taking a place next to the merchant in the ragged clothes. This response made Reuben smile, but that action only highlighted the wound on his face.

"Did you once live here?" Reuben asked turning to look at Tristan.

"I lived near here not long ago. There were people staying here who are very important to me. I need to know what happened to them," replied Tristan.

He kept his eyes forward at the destruction around him, whilst also attempting to keep his voice level. He wasn't good at hiding the emotion in his voice, so he made himself raise his voice where it would be tempted to break.

"I wasn't here long before this all happened. I was just passing through a couple of nights to trade my wares for things that I could possibly trade in Malancore. The people here were more than generous and very kind; it's horrible what happened to them," said Reuben looking around at the destruction as well, but his eyes ended on the dirt.

"What did happen?"

"It was in the night; I heard screaming coming from outside. I was staying in the inn yonder, so I looked out the window to see men dressed in black with terrible white masks covering the top halves of their faces. They dragged people out of their houses screaming, themselves laughing horribly. They went door to door dragging people into the square in their night clothes. I only evaded their notice by lifting up the floor tiles and hiding under them. The masked men said something about the Phantoms of Shadow and another thing about a blood offering. They then proceeded to throw the older folk into the church and other tied the children and young women. That when the burning started," said Reuben darkly looking into the ground as he told Tristan this.

"They burned it all? With everyone inside?" asked Tristan resisting the tears that threatened to well up in his eyes, instead opting to let the emotion turn to anger.

"Starting with the church, they threw fire into it,

consuming it with flame. I can still hear the screams in my head. They then went, building to building, burning them down. I only barely got out, but as you can see a burning beam fell on my face, but at least I have my life. Then they left with their prisoners heading south." replied Reuben soberly, pointing to the order of the buildings they burned.

"At least you have your life," muttered Tristan his eyes burning as they stared into the ground.

"I have nothing left; that's why I've been here the past two days. Treating my wound as best as I can and thinking about what to do next," said Reuben looking around at the landscape but then fixing his eyes on Tristan, who was still glaring at the dirt.

"How dare you be the one who escaped with your life!" shouted Tristan.

He drew his sword once again. The action made Reuben startled his face full of shock.

"You have no right to be the one who lived when they died!" he screamed with all his lungs pushing the man down with his foot, his anger stirring up more with every word, his cheeks burning with rage.

"You should have burnt with them!" he screamed amidst the begging and whimpering coming from Reuben, bringing his sword up in two hands his blade point down.

"That's enough Tristan."

He heard a Pickish voice to his left, and he turned to see Joshua on an old brown horse, his eyes face set and grim. Tristan felt his arms go weak and his sword falling to his side, and his boot lifted from the man's chest. Reuben got to his feet immediately and scurried as quickly as possible to Joshua, trying to keep the man between himself and the young man who nearly ran him through with a sword. Tristan's legs gave way as he fell back onto the base of the tree, holding his face in his hands.

He wanted to cry, he wanted to burst into tears, and release everything within him in tears, but he couldn't. These were his last family, and he'd promised he would come back to them. To them. Not their ashes. He couldn't cry; he was too numb. All he could do was feel his hand going to the Oakleaf in his pocket and clutching it. It was all collapsing around him. Tristan didn't even notice Joshua limping to his side, using a stick instead of his hobbling like before. Joshua sat down next to him, and the two of them sat in silence.

"What's your next step Tristan?" asked Joshua.

Something struck him. The thing he needed to do. He sat up taking the necklace from his pocket and put it on, the oakleaf coming to his chest and he set his face forward.

"I'm going to find whoever did this, kill them and rescue the people they took," he resolved, his eyes forward to the buildings, with each second, more determined with his resolution.

"Would it change your mind if I told you that won't give you the peace that you hope it will bring you?" asked Joshua himself looking forward at the buildings.

"It wouldn't."

"I thought not. In that case you'll need this," he said.

Joshua took a small purse from his side and placed it into Tristan's hand. Tristan could feel the weight and sounds of coin in it, and looked up to Joshua a little surprised.

"This is too generous," Tristan insisted offering it back, but Joshua simply closed his hand around it and pushed it back.

"For the man who saved my life, hardly. You be careful out there Tristan, don't trust anyone and keep yourself guarded. Set a line in your head, a time, or an action that you won't cross, otherwise you will spend your life on revenge, and that's a life wasted," said Joshua looking at him deeply, his eyes still soft, but completely serious in every word.

"Thank you," Tristan whispered, weighing the purse in his hand and then stuffed it into his pocket.

"When are you planning on leaving?" asked Joshua using his stick to get to his feet, but Tristan was at his side when he attempted it, and they got him upright together.

"As soon as I can. I'll travel light so it'll be easier on the horse weight-wise, but I don't plan on seeing the sights," he replied going to help Joshua move but he put up his hand to stop him, and limped forward on his stick, going towards his old horse that Reuben still cowering behind it.

"I thought so. I actually think he'll prefer running to having my weight on him at all hours," laughed Joshua, and Tristan tried to laugh with him, but all that came out was a hoarse choke that he attempted to turn into a cough.

"What about you and Rosa?"

"Well - I think we'll stick around here for a little at least until my leg fully heals or after she's had the baby. We may need to use some of the animals in the now abandoned farms for food, but we'll manage - we always have. Then after that, I want to move somewhere we can grow our family where they won't be affected by war or Kings," he replied looking up at the grey sky. He actually looked content.

This made Tristan smile a sad smile, knowing that wasn't something he'd feel for some time.

"Well I wish you the best, I really do. You deserve a peaceful life," said Tristan forcing himself to keep his smile towards Joshua.

"You do too Tristan, I'm just afraid you'll realise that too late," observed Joshua smiling back, and then turned to approach Reuben.

Tristan decided it was time to leave. It didn't take long for Tristan to get the white horse he had decided to call Ulysses ready for riding. He had enough provisions in his rucksack to last him a couple of weeks, and he could make the money

Joshua had given him go far. He put his chainmail shirt into the paddle bag and some of his other heavier items. He had a feeling that he would need it wherever he was going. He would get Isabella back; he would see her again. Tristan had to banish the thought going round in his head that she was one of those burned in the church, because she had to be alive. She had to be.

Tristan waited before he left to see Joshua off, heading back down the road that his old home was built along. Joshua had seemingly taken pity on Reuben as the merchant walked next to the old brown horse, sometimes having to jog a little to keep pace with him. Tristan watched them until they were out of sight, keeping Ulysses' head in his hand and he whispered to the horse nothing in particular. He wasn't familiar with horses and their ways, but Ulysses seemed like he would make very good company. He didn't ask questions, he didn't care what he was doing, he would just be there for the ride, and Tristan needed someone like that now.

The sky was getting greyer when he set off, but Tristan didn't mind; he'd get a few good miles before he had to camp. He pushed Ulysses to go faster and faster, leaving Tindale behind him, but the numbness stayed. Tristan didn't have a large plan, or anything fancy like that. He was going to kill the men in the white masks if it was the last thing he did, and a part of him hoped it was. His sword was at his side, his long dagger behind his belt and the necklace bouncing on his neck from the motion made by the horse. That necklace was a reminder to him, a way he'd never forget. He was going to find Isabella again, and heaven help the man who tried to stop him.

# CHAPTER 15

## THE WOLVES ARE STILL RUNNING

*T*he stables attached to the side of the Smiling Duck weren't large by any stretch of the imagination, only boasting three stalls for travellers to keep their horses, but it was dry and there was enough hay to satisfy most animals kept there. The most important feature of it at this time for Pip was the silence. It was just him and Izzy in there, and he felt like he could finally breathe for a little. He knew once he left, most time would be just the two of them, yet it was still nice to have this moment.

The last two weeks of recovery had been a blur for him and considering Jacklin had told him that rest was so important, she had certainly kept him on his feet. As soon as he could stand, they had a party in the Smiling Duck which the entire town stead had attended. There were many smiling faces, and laughing, and lots of glances in his direction. He stuck with Peter and Amys, but people continually came up to him, saying their thanks to him, and he'd always say something small in return, which they'd smile about and then shuffle away.

After that, he had tried to build back his fitness, but it was hard to do when Jacklin had many people who wanted to talk to him about this and that, giving him their personal and proper thanks. He'd had the opportunity to meet Pip the cat and had the scratches to prove it. As much as he could, he trained with Carlos, building his strength up, but even then, men would come up to him and ask him how to use certain weapons.

Yet throughout it all, he had the persistent feeling that he was time to leave. It would happen particularly at night times because that's when he was alone and left to his thoughts. He had unfinished business he needed to attend to and every day he waited, things could be getting worse. The wolves were still running and there could be worse things in the north. That's why he packed his things and was now standing in the stable scratching Izzy's nose.

"Are you sure you want to leave; I could always use a few extra hands to help in the tavern. I could even try and find a job for you elsewhere?" asked Jacklin walking into the stable, a stable bag in her hands that was filled with provisions.

"I have to leave," he insisted leading Izzy forward, looking over to Jacklin who looked a little disappointed but very much unsurprised as she put the bag over Izzy's back.

"I know - I just wanted to double check," she said giving a smile in his direction and then moved to Izzy's front and leading her out of the stable.

They both walked out into the early morning. He knew it had to be in the morning when he left. Pip didn't want a goodbye party, so all there was waiting for him as they emerged from the stable was Peter and Amys, both smiling at him as they rubbed the tiredness out of his eyes. When Amys saw him, she ran up to Pip and gave his leg a big hug, wrapping both her arms around them. This did warrant a smile from him and he patted her head fondly.

"I'm going to miss you Pip, I really will," Amys smiled up

at him, and Pip got down on his knees to be at her level. He pulled out a little wooden block he'd carved into a leaf and put it into her hands.

"Just something to remind you of me when I'm gone," he said, and she held it in her hands in total awe at the thing. She then gave him a big hug that nearly threw him off balance completely, and all he could think to do was pat her slightly awkwardly. When she eventually let him go, he stood up as quickly as he could, but he tried to give her a smile. Then Peter set forward the sword he had given him in his hands.

"I figured I should give this back to you. I don't think I can be a man like you," he said his eyes filled with genuineness as he held his weapon towards Pip.

"Then don't be," he replied plainly and took the reins from Jacklin.

"What do you mean?" he protested, walking in front of Pip, still holding out his sword for the other man to take.

"You are a good man and you never need a sword for that. But it might be useful, and if a few more good men had swords, there won't be any need for men like me - it's yours," he replied looking everywhere but Peter's eyes as he spoke and the man looked forward for a second, and then pulled it closer to himself resolutely.

Pip then led Izzy into the main street, his leaving party remaining on the porch of the Smiling Duck, waving at him as he climbed on her back. He was never good at goodbyes, so he gave them a wave and his best attempt at a smile. Then he turned back and kicked Izzy to move forward slowly at a trot. He was heading north, and he didn't know what would come next, but he knew where he was heading. There were things that were unfinished that needed to be laid to rest for good. He felt the sword at his side, the long dagger behind his back and the pouch that held the broken pieces of a neck-lace. He had a promise to keep.

THE END

# ACKNOWLEDGMENTS

Thank you to my wonderful mother for editing this book.

Thank you to Jacob Hobson for the cover art.

Thank you to Newcastle University for giving me four random weeks off in April.

Printed in Great Britain
by Amazon